At Your Service Copiers

By Michael S. Modzelewski

This book is dedicated to my lovely wife and our incredible daughter. Their patience and encouragement throughout its writing has helped turn a dream into a reality.

This book is also dedicated to the talented professionals in the service industry. Whether you repair or support the repair of the international space station, a toaster or anything in between. Your skill, dedication, and hard work help keep this world running and it is appreciated.

Thank You

Cover and graphics design by Michael S. Modzelewski and Bill Defrance, prepress@actiongraphicsnj.com

CONTENTS

Chapter 1 – In the Beginning

Ron sat down in his new office for the first time and thought, "I've waited a long time for this!" Ron had previously managed a small team of technicians for At Your Service Copiers in a small town in Illinois. It had become boring, repetitious and was starting to drive him crazy. The most exciting thing that ever happened there was when an office romance between one of his technicians and an operator went sour. He had accepted a transfer to New York and was now fulfilling his dream of managing in a big city. He looked out of his fortieth floor window and thought, "Finally, here at last!"

His new Boss Chuck had already explained to Ron that he was replacing a manager who just quit one day, for personal reasons.

There was a knock on the door, Chuck rushed in before Ron could say anything and asked him, "Well Ron, are you ready to meet your new team?"

Ron enthusiastically replied, "Raring and ready sir!"

Chuck thought to himself, "That will change."

Chuck led Ron through the dispatch room, along the way a few people recognized him as the new manager and told him, "Good luck, you'll need it," and "Poor guy." He briefly met Renee, his team's dispatcher. Renee tried to tell him, "We need to talk right away," but was quickly cut off by Chuck who replied, "Not now Renee." As Ron was being led past her, Ron turned and told her, "I promise, we'll talk later."

Ron was starting to feel uncomfortable with Chuck's behavior and felt like he was being dragged along to his new team, perhaps before he could change his mind. Ron's instincts had usually served him well in the past and he thought, "Oh crap, what did I get myself into?"

As they approached the meeting room door, Ron heard what sounded like a party going on. He could hear loud music blaring and people yelling in the room.

Ron grabbed Chuck by the arm, spun him around and bluntly told him, "I want to know right now, what the hell is going on. From the beginning you've been vague as hell Chuck, what haven't you been telling me?"

Chuck looked up at Ron and replied, "Alright, you're right, you should know before you open that door. You're now in charge of the worst team of misfits I've ever met. I'm sorry I didn't tell you earlier but you probably would never have taken this assignment if I told you the whole truth, I'm desperate."

They arrived at the door; Chuck opened it and had Ron walk through first. Ron heard someone yell, "Yeah, fresh meat!"

Ron quickly glanced around the room and saw guys with their feet on the table, talking on their phones. Everyone was yelling over one another but through it all there was one guy fast asleep, oblivious to everything.

Chuck quickly tried to call the meeting to order but had no control over the guy's.
Ron tried to gain control and announced, "Children, shut the hell up, I'm your new boss!"

With that, Ron was bombarded by a barrage of balled up papers and a couple of the guy's had cans of silly string they started spraying all over him. As the silly string started covering his face, Ron caught a glimpse of someone holding a fire extinguisher. He cleared some of the string from his face just in time to see it spray but was able to maneuver himself out of the way. Ron finally lost it and lunged at the tech who had tried to spray him. He grabbed the fire extinguisher from the tech, gave him a short burst then pointed it at the team.

Ron told them, "The next one who say's or does anything gets it!"

Suddenly, one of the techs yelled out, "Ah-hah!" and Ron let him have it!

Chuck told Ron, "Welcome to the dog pound," and quickly left the room. The room suddenly erupted into chaos again, most of the techs started making barking and howling noises. Ron sprayed some of the techs that were closest to him and then; finally, silence filled the room.

Ron took advantage of the silence and told his new team, "What the hell is wrong with you people, are you all retarded?" One tech started to say, "We're the dog…" but Ron sprayed him with the fire extinguisher before he could finish.

Ron continued, "Anyone else!" No one said anything and Ron added, "Good, now listen up! You butt-holes are mine now and I'm not taking this crap from any of you!" He added, "If you don't think you can conduct yourselves like adult, professional human beings then quit now and save me the trouble of firing you!"

The techs were still silent so Ron asked them, "Who the hell is my specialist?" Someone directly to his right raised his hand and introduced himself as Al.

Ron announced, "This excuse for a meeting is over, get the hell out of here and get to work. Al, meet me in my office, right now!"

Ron opened the door and saw at least a half dozen people standing there; they had been listening through the door and were now applauding and trying to high five him on his way out. Ron was angry and rushed past them. He found the bathroom and started cleaning up then realized his hands were trembling; it had been a long time since he was that upset about anything. He couldn't decide who he was angrier at, his new team of misfits or Chuck.

"Ah hell," he thought, "They're all butt holes!"

He added, "This is what I'm moving my wife and daughter half way across the country for, I've got to be freaking nuts." Then he thought about how much he had wanted this assignment and figured, "I'll give this place a few weeks, I'm not putting them through a move like this until I'm sure I'm staying."

After cleaning up and calming himself down he made it back to his office. Al was there waiting for him, Ron closed the door and laid into him right away.

He said, "What the hell is wrong with you guy's."

Al replied, "Ron, you have every reason to be upset but understand, there are some decent guy's in that room.

There may not be many and it's been a long time since they've been able to show it but they're there. If it helps, you caught the team by surprise today, they're all crapping their pants right now."

Al put his hand out to Ron and told him, "Please believe me Ron, I'm on your side. I've been waiting a long time for someone to come along and bitch slap these knuckleheads, welcome aboard."

Ron shook Al's hand and apologized for coming down on him so hard.

Ron and Al sat and talked for at least an hour as Al explained the team's history. The phone rang constantly and people were continuously knocking on the door but Ron ignored it all, he knew he had to come up to speed quickly. Ron listened intently to Al as he described some of his teammates. First, Ron wanted to know about the tech who was asleep through the whole meeting, Al explained that was Stu, one of the laziest of the bunch, he dresses like a slob and does his job only when he has too.

Ron told Al, "He'll probably be first on the list of people to go."

Al replied, "Good luck with that, his parents own a third of our stock, besides, Stu isn't even close to being the worst of the bunch." Al went on to describe a pair of real losers, Frank and Tom. Al added, "Tom was the guy with the fire extinguisher, you may not have seen it but Frank had one too, he backed down once you got the one from Tom, they wanted to ambush you."

Ron replied sarcastically, "I can't thank you guys enough for backing me up Al."

Al replied, "Sorry Ron, this has become the norm around here, nothing new with this crew. Al went on, "Tom and Frank work closely together and do little or no work, I almost think Frank runs interference for Tom. No one's been able to tell them anything, the last manager seemed to just give up and quit rather than deal with them."

Ron told Al, "That's funny; Chuck told me something similar but left out a lot of details."

Al replied, "I can see why, Chuck couldn't get anyone to take charge of this group for a long time. I guess you guys in Illinois haven't heard of us yet. Chuck tried everywhere to get a manager to take over, they all laughed in his face. If it helps, I think he did good, what you did today needed to be done a long time ago. There are a few guy's on the team who left the meeting really happy this morning."

Just then, Al's phone rang and it was Renee. Al picked it up and was told she desperately needed him to take some service calls. Ron agreed it was best so they decided to continue their conversation another day.

Ron spent the rest of the morning answering his phone calls. One by one the attacks continued and every call was from an angry sales rep or customer. They all sounded the same, "I placed a call over two hours ago, where's my service rep, this machine is down everyday, I want it out of here, now!"

He spoke to one customer three times and almost laughed in the guys face, the customer, Bruce, sounded more like a woman than most of the women he had met. Bruce said he owned an assertiveness training school and Ron muttered under his breath, "Good luck with that." Bruce overheard Ron and got upset with him. Ron was able to blow him off and told him, "You misunderstood, I said, I heard that."

After he finally got the customer off of the phone, he thought about his office in Illinois. Right about now he'd be going for an early lunch, probably meet up with a few of his techs or better yet meet up with his wife and daughter at Chucky Cheese.

Ron picked up the phone and decided to call his wife Angela, she always knew how to cheer him up. The phone rang a few times and just as Ron was ready to give up, she answered, "Hello,"

Ron replied, "Hey gorgeous, miss me?"

"Oh Ron," she replied, "I've been wanting to call you all morning. I didn't want to bother you on your first day, I miss you terribly honey, how are you?"

Ron asked about their daughter Katie, who was in kindergarten then explained a little about the meeting and how his new team must have been graduates from the animal house. He told her all about Chuck and the fast one he pulled on him.

Ron added, "Chuck really suckered me in. Not to worry though, I think I can handle it."

Angela replied, "Ron, please don't overdue it out there, promise me you'll call your sponsor, he called here a couple of times to see how you're doing. And find a meeting out there, please, promise."

Ron replied, "Of course I will honey, you know I love you and Katie more than anything. Hopefully you'll be out here in a few weeks and we can get back to normal. After a few minutes, Angela had to go and pick up Katie from school so they said their goodbyes for now. Ron promised to call later that night.

After hanging up, Ron thought for a moment, he knew his wife was right. The last thing he needed was a relapse; he worked too hard to stay sober the last few years.

He looked up at his clock and realized it was time for lunch then realized he never caught up with his dispatcher, Renee.

He got up from his desk and realized that for the last five minutes he had heard silence and thought, "I could get used to that," then sat back down and enjoyed the quiet for a few more minutes.

He eventually got up and made his way to the dispatch area. He was stopped a number of times along the way by other managers and sales people, all wishing him well and congratulating him on his show of force at the meeting. Ron made it to Renee's desk and found her on the phone with a customer; Renee looked up and rolled her eyes in disgust. After five minutes she finally got off of the phone, told Ron it was the assertiveness training guy and they both sighed.

Renee added, "You're going to learn to really despise that guy Ron, he calls every twenty minutes until someone gets over there."

Ron replied, "Anyway, sorry for not catching up with you earlier, come on, let me buy my dispatcher lunch." Ron told the other dispatchers, "Cover Renee's calls for awhile, we'll be in a meeting."

Renee was a young, attractive girl, probably in her mid twenties. She had been with At your Service Copiers for at least five years but transferred to New York from Atlanta Georgia only a few years ago. Fortunately for Ron's team she had maintained her sweet sounding southern drawl and could help calm a techs nerves on the most stressful of days, if she chose to. Ron found Renee to be a sweet girl who preferred to be easy going but because of her job, she learned to adapt and could be a real hard ass when she needed to. She described to Ron some of the details of his team. He was starting to put together that his predecessor was driven out of his job by an unmanageable group of techs.

She told him, "He was just too nice a guy for this bunch; they all need a kick in the rear end!" She added, "That customer that keeps calling every twenty minutes, the one that sounds like a girl, his tech is Greg. The guy never shows up when you need him, never calls his customers. Then I have to bust my butt and find someone else to take his calls. Usually I have to bother Brad or John but that's not fair, they have their own work to do."

Ron asked, "Who's Brad and John?"

Renee replied, "You'll love those two, they grew up together in Brooklyn, joined the Marines together and now work here together. I hear they were in combat together during Desert Storm. I don't know what I'd do if it wasn't for them, they've bailed me out about as much as Al.

Ron had been taking notes then stopped and asked Renee, "So who else does any real work around here?"

Renee replied, "That's it, Al, Brad and John."

Ron looked stunned and responded, "You mean out of that whole room of guys there are only three who actually work?"

Renee told Ron, "I'm afraid so, we'd be dead if we didn't get help from other teams once in awhile, but they're getting tired of helping us, we've turned into the laughing stock of the city."

Ron asked about Tom and Frank, Renee explained they were the most obnoxious pair of techs she'd ever met. No one can tell them anything and they almost never answer her calls, Frank does but only once in awhile. They practically dare managers to challenge them. Ron asked Renee, "How so, can you be specific."

Renee thought for a moment then told Ron, "I remember more than once calling Tom to take a call in his territory. Tom wouldn't be dispatched but would tell me to leave him alone, I'm busy. When I called his manager, the manager would call him, then call me back and tell me just leave Tom alone, get someone else to take the call. It's like Tom has something over these managers."

Ron could tell Renee was getting emotional the more she went on. He changed the subject for a while and finished lunch on a positive note. Ron did assure her he'd find a way to change things, he added, "Just give me a little time and keep me in the loop."

They returned to the office and Ron spent the afternoon going over the records of his techs. He couldn't believe it but there were no documented problems with any of them, not one tech had been written up, ever.

The next few days were spent going from one account after another. Ron and Al showed up every morning and waited until the techs showed up where they were supposed to be dispatched. They documented a majority of the team, some were coming in two or three hours late, some weren't coming in at all. By the end of the first week Ron had zeroed in on a few techs he knew he would have to deal with, first on the list was Tom. Ron tried calling him but never reached him or received a call back. He asked Renee where he was dispatched and Renee replied, "You're kidding, right."

Ron wondered, "How can I get this guys attention?"

Ron knew Tom had been with At Your Service for at least five years so he had Renee leave a message for Tom stating there was a special company bonus available to long-term employees. Within a few hours Tom contacted Ron and asked about the bonus, Ron instructed Tom to come up to the office and fill out some paperwork.

The next morning, Ron arrived at the office bright and early, hopeful but doubtful Tom might come in early. Ron was nervous about how his meeting with Tom would go but preferred to not let the anticipation drag on all day.

He was greeted by Chuck's secretary, Mildred who explained that Chuck had arranged for interviews to be conducted that day. Mildred was in her sixties and close to retirement, she had been Chuck's secretary from day one. Her desk appeared unchanged since the day she started. Somehow Mildred found an old style rotary phone that worked with the new phone systems and she refused to learn how to operate a computer. Everyone in the vicinity complained when she used her ancient typewriter because of the awful racket it made, but had learned it was pointless to complain.

She explained that Chuck had lined up some solid candidates for tech positions and asked that Ron sit in on some of the interviews, perhaps pick out a couple of technicians, anticipating some firings on his team. Ron was assigned to sit in with another manager, Bill on a potential candidate named Mike.

Bill was also a manager at AYS and responsible for a team of technicians on the west side of town. Like Ron, he too was in his mid thirties but divorced a number of years ago after the job took its toll on his marriage. Bill was very hard working but had become frustrated with the way things were run in the office. In order to survive, he had recently learned to coast through the insanity rather than change it. Most of Bill's techs were good workers but he too had his share of screw-ups, it was a challenge but somehow he was able to make it work.

Their new candidate Mike was in his early twenties with blond hair and blue eyes, he had been honorably discharged from the United States Air Force only a month earlier. Although Mike was having a great time catching up with his old friends, partying all hours of the night in the city, funds were getting low and he very much needed the job.

Mike arrived at the office a little early and was asked to wait in the dispatch area while the managers prepared for the interview. He was amazed at all the activity going on. He had gotten used to working at a remote radar site in the Nevada desert and was excited to see all the activity.

There were at least ten dispatchers in cubicles, on the phone, all seeming to be saying the same thing. "How can I help you, Sorry for the delay, we'll have someone there as quickly as possible." There was also a constant flow of traffic through the area, people with tool carts, boxes and paperwork, all rushing through at once. A lot more exciting than watching cactus grow and sagebrush blowing in the wind, then he thought, "I could get used to this."

He was eventually called in to Chuck's office and the interview began. He was bombarded with questions like, "If a customer told you he wanted to throw his copier out of the window, what would you tell him? His machine has been down all day and he's upset, how would you deal with him? It's five o'clock and your dispatcher has an irate customer, she needs you to head over there, what do you tell her? And the questions went on and on. Without much experience in customer service but lots of military discipline, Mike managed his way through that part of the interview. Chuck very subtly commented on Mike's accent, which still had a touch of New York but also had a southwestern twang. Mike explained that he had been away in Nevada and joked, "You haven't lived till you've heard a New York accent and the word y'all combined. The managers all had a good laugh and Mike noticed Ron taking notes, he was hopeful they were positive. They moved on to the technical part of the interview, copiers were a lot different than a radar set, less complicated but the wiring diagrams were laid out much differently. Bill gave Mike a number of wiring diagrams, tools and parts to handle. Chuck commented that he seemed a little nervous and was fumbling through some of the wiring but had him continue.

Towards the end of the interview there was a knock at the door, it was Chuck's secretary and she was looking for Ron, apparently Tom had arrived for their meeting. Chuck and Bill continued the interview while Ron excused himself and headed to his office just a few doors down.

Tom was in Ron's office when Ron arrived. Ron could see why so many people were reluctant to deal with him; Tom was huge and obviously spent a lot of time in the gym. Ron took a seat at his desk and explained, "First, there is no special bonus, I…"

Tom cut Ron off before he could finish and told him, "You brought me up here for nothing, had me waiting around like an idiot, do you know how busy I am?"

Ron continued, "I'm glad you brought that up Tom, that's exactly why I called you up here. If you're so busy I have to ask you, what are you busy doing? I spent a couple of mornings at some of your sites waiting for you to show up and you never did. I've called you and you've never responded, dispatch can't get you to take calls, what the hell do you do all day?"

Tom shot right back, "You have some nerve, spying on me, you think after five years at this place I'd get some respect, I've paid my dues, dealt with your stupid customers, what the hell do you want from me?"

Ron replied, "How about an honest day's work!"

Ron could tell Tom was getting angry and thought, "Good, maybe he'll see how everyone else feels!"

Ron continued, "So Tom, talk to me, what do you do all day?"

Tom replied, "I don't have to tell you squat, you're here a week and trying to give me orders already, who do you think you are?"

Ron replied, "Your boss Tom and if you don't cut the crap I'm the boss who's going to fire you, right now, understand!"

Tom became noticeably agitated for a moment and Ron reached into his pocket for the can of pepper spray he had stashed, just in case. With no warning, Tom sprang from his chair and reached for Ron on the other side of his desk. Tom landed on Ron's desk with a thud, face down and stopped dead in his tracks. He resembled a beached whale and was moaning in agony. As Tom looked up, Ron showed Tom the can of pepper spray and asked him,

"Am I going to need to use this?"

Tom replied, "No, can you help me up though?"

Ron replied, "Where does it hurt?"

Tom responded, "My back!"

Ron told him, "No, but stay there while I call an ambulance for you."

Ron went outside and had Mildred call for an ambulance. She started dialing with her rotary phone and Ron had to laugh, and then thought, "This could take awhile."

Chuck excused himself from the interview, came in to Ron's office and immediately asked Ron, "What did you do!"

Tom quickly replied, "He's a bully sir, look what he did to me."

Chuck looked at Ron and saw him grinning from ear to ear. He knew Tom was full of crap and replied, "So Tom, you expect me to believe that Ron picked up a big guy like you and threw you on his desk, is that right?"

Al arrived in Ron's office just as Chuck had finished speaking.

Tom replied, "Yeah, the pervert was trying to have sex with me!"

Chuck and Ron could no longer contain themselves and busted out laughing.

Al asked them, "What did I miss?"

Chuck replied, "Like I always say, "The bigger they are the harder they fall!"

The paramedics arrived and started placing Tom on a stretcher. As they were leaving, Ron leaned down and whispered into Tom's ear, "By the way, you're fired!"

Al asked Ron, "What did you do!"

Ron replied, "Got lucky I guess!"

Chuck added, "You realize he'll probably take us to court."

Ron pointed to the teddy bear on his desk and explained, "My daughter gave me that before I came here, it's her nanny cam. I recorded the whole thing."

Al added, "I've got to see this, should I get the popcorn!"

While all of this was going on, Bill and Mike had left Chucks office and saw Tom being taken out of Ron's office on a stretcher. Mike was stunned and was having second thoughts about working there, especially when he saw everyone giddy with laughter while a tech was lying there in pain.

Bill chuckled and told Mike, "Good news kid, looks like we have an opening."

Chuck noticed Mike standing there and asked Ron, "So what do you think about this guy Ron, think he can help you?"

Ron thought about it for a moment and remembered his only two working techs were former military, maybe it was an omen that Mike showed up today of all days. Ron looked at Mike and asked, "What do you think Mike, do you want to work for me?"

Mike thought about what he had just witnessed and asked himself, "Is this guy crazy?" Then he remembered his financial situation, funds were running out quickly so

Mike pointed to Tom on the stretcher and asked, "How's your medical?"

Chapter 2 – The Transition

After a couple of weeks, Ron found himself settling into his new position as well as anyone could. He and Al continued to show up at accounts without warning and monitoring the whereabouts of the techs throughout the day. In the weeks that followed the firing of Tom, Ron had let go of two more techs. Oddly enough it didn't impact the workload at all, the techs he fired never did any work anyway. Unfortunately Chuck advised Ron that he had to wait before letting go of anyone else. Company policy prevented management from firing more than a couple of techs per year and Ron already exceeded that with three. That meant Ron was stuck with Stu, Greg and Frank for awhile, Ron could not believe there were lazier techs than them. They did seem to be working a little harder lately and Ron thought, "Maybe they'll come around after all."

In the district, Ron was beginning to be treated like a rock star. After Tom was seen being carried out of Ron's office on a stretcher, the rumor mill ran riot throughout the company. Depending on whom you heard the story from; Ron was a former green beret who took Tom out with one punch or a kung fu master who easily forced Tom into submission. Either way, Ron was trying to stay humble and not let it all go to his head but it was becoming difficult. The entire district was treating him like a hero and he was starting to think, "Maybe I am!"

As things were starting to go well with the job it was another story back home in Illinois.

Ron was on the phone with his wife when Al knocked on his door. They were both upset, the house in Illinois wasn't selling as quickly as they had planned and they both missed each other more than they ever realized they could.

Even Ron's daughter was starting to act out, Katie would break into crying spells screaming, "I want my daddy, where's my daddy?" She would stand on the sofa and look out of the window, waiting for Ron's car to pull up in the driveway, expecting him to take her to the park or for ice cream like he used to. Ron missed the way she laughed when he smashed their ice cream cones together and made a new flavor. He would say, "Smoosh," and Katie would usually laugh and reply something like, "You silly daddy!" The word had become part of her early vocabulary.

Angela was becoming increasingly concerned as Ron wasn't going to meetings anymore. He would tell her he's fine and had no cravings but lots of work. She was happy for him being able to live out his dream and find the success he appeared to be having but couldn't help but worry, Ron only had a few years sobriety under his belt. His sponsor told him he'd probably be alright moving to New York but it was imperative he get connected to a new AA group as soon as he got there. Ron asked Angela to be patient and reasoned the house would sell eventually; he would try to take a week off as soon as he could and light a fire under the real estate agents butt.

He added, "Please don't worry about me honey, you have enough to worry about out there. I promise I'll start looking for some meetings in the area right away.

They hung up and Ron told Al to come in. Al noticed Ron seemed a little upset and asked him if everything was alright.

Ron explained, "Problems at home, we were hoping the house in Illinois would be sold by now and it's not. We were counting on being together again by now and were not, it just sucks!"

Al replied, "I think I can imagine how you feel, I know how bad I miss my wife and kids when I have to go for training at the main office, I sympathize completely. Can Chuck cut you loose for awhile? You've already done so much to help the group."

Ron responded, "Great minds think alike Al, You must've been reading my mind. I'm going to talk to Chuck as soon as this meeting is over."

This morning, Ron had arranged a meeting with his techs. Mike, the new hire had completed his training last week and was expected in the office any minute. Ron and Al couldn't wait; they were desperate for some new talent and were hoping Mike would be a keeper. Ron thought about the day Mike was hired and chuckled, "He must think I'm a psycho," Remembering that Tom was wheeled out on a stretcher during his interview.

After a few weeks in Atlanta, Mike was in no hurry to return home, the nightlife and southern hospitality of Georgia women were more than enough to make him forget about missing New York. He was almost ready to ask for a transfer but knew better. He was told his district had paid a lot of money for his training so thought it a bad idea. The training class was great, but he knew he still had a lot to learn. His instructors stressed the need for teamwork and he hoped his new teammates felt the same.

After fighting his way through rush hour crowds on the subway, he made his way to the office, up the elevator and finally back at the reception area where he saw Gertie, the receptionist from his interview.

Gertie was an upper middle aged woman, a little on the heavy side but attractive and took excellent care of herself. She was always impeccably dressed and was rumored to be dating Albert, the lobby security guard. No one knew for sure as Gertie was discrete and knew how to keep a secret. This was fortunate for everyone in the office considering she knew everything that was going on at all times.

It really only felt like yesterday since Mike was here. Gertie remembered Mike, welcomed him back and asked him how training went. Mike was reluctant to tell her much about the nightlife. He thought he wouldn't last one day if he told anyone much about Atlanta. There were mornings when Mike made it back to his hotel with barely enough time to change and get to training. He cordially explained the trip was nice but there was just so much work.

Gertie replied, "It's a shame you didn't make use of the nightlife, some of the guys have returned with some great stories." She had a really sly smile and Mike wondered if she couldn't tell him a few stories of her own.

As they were speaking, Bill the manager who interviewed Mike approached him and said he had been assigned to Ron's group. He explained that Ron had been making a name for himself while he was away in training and had let go of a couple more techs. Mike asked Bill if there were any more ambulances called in and Bill laughed, and then told Mike, "The incident with Tom was not what it appeared to be, Ron never got violent with anyone. In fact he's been very professional and was anxiously waiting for you; he's hoping you'll be the start of his team rebuild."

Bill brought Mike to Ron's office, knocked on the door and was greeted by Al. Al and Ron both asked Mike about his training experience and explained to Mike how glad they were to have him on the team.

Ron added, "I'm really kind of new to this place myself Mike, I've been learning as I go and can promise you'll never have a dull moment."

Bill left as Mike, Ron and Al made their way to the meeting. As the door opened he thought he was in a frat house or something. Guys were throwing balled up papers back and forth, and two of the guys were throwing paper airplanes with skull and crossbones at each other. One guy was fast asleep through it all, but had spitballs all over him. As they came through the door it continued unimpeded. Mike had one of the airplanes launched his way, he ducked and someone yelled, "Nuke him."

Just then he was bombarded with a barrage of balled up paper from everywhere. When it stopped he looked up and was hit right between the eyes with one of the paper airplanes.

Everyone exploded in laughter and yelled, "Hi Mike!"

Ron turned to Mike and said, "Welcome to the dog pound, you should see how they welcomed me," but never did elaborate.

Mike took a seat next to the guy with all the spitballs all over him who was finally waking up. He looked up at Mike with one eye open and asked who he was, then wondered out loud if he was in the wrong meeting again. After a minute or so things settled down and Ron told everyone to listen up.

He said that with the loss of a few techs it was necessary to start realigning the territories. They would start two weeks from now and was open to suggestions as of today. Everyone started saying they wanted Fusia, Ron quickly replied who ever got Fusia would also have to take

Phoenix. That quieted things down and Mike wondered what that was about.

The next order of business was a trial at dress down Fridays. At the moment the dress code called for dress pants, dress shirt and tie. He explained they would lighten up and allow Dockers and a collared knit or dress shirt, no tie.

Everyone including Mike heavily applauded and started taking off their ties.

Ron quickly stopped them and told the guys, "Before you start getting naked, the dress down code will be a trial and would start next week, if it is abused it will be taken away in a heartbeat."

Just then, the entire team looked at Stu, the spitball guy. He looked up, noticed everyone staring at him and replied, "What?"

Ron again introduced Mike and said we would also have another new tech in a few weeks, a woman named Kelly and added she was to be treated with the utmost respect or else.

They went through a few other topics like vacation schedules for the month and other things. At the end of the meeting Mike was told he would travel with Al for a couple of weeks. Before Mike could pick up any bad habits from the group, Ron wanted Mike to be broken in by his specialist. Al was a great tech who was professional and seasoned. He could be counted on to teach Mike some good habits and also evaluate Mike's skill level and temperament.

Ron wrapped up the meeting and everyone quickly left the room. Al brought Mike into the dispatch area where he met his dispatcher Renee; she was extremely busy so after a quick exchange of pleasantries they headed for the locker room. Al explained to Mike that although Renee was a good dispatcher, part of her job was to keep the techs moving in order to keep response times down. He added, "Don't take it personal if she calls to verbally bitch slap you to quickly finish a call and take another one. Last week she called a tech and told him to wake up and take a call. It just so happened to be Stu, the spitball guy next to you in the meeting, who probably was behind a machine sleeping."

They made their way into the locker room where there was a small canyon of lockers, each with someone's name on them. Each locker belonged to an individual tech and was filled with their parts and tools. Al explained to Mike that he might end up with a locker here or possibly one at an account, it had not been decided. If he were lucky his locker would be at a customer's site that he would be responsible for. To have a locker in the office meant you would always be under the scrutiny of managers and dispatchers. Not only that, but if you were nearby when a tech was needed ASAP you would be quickly dragged into a problem.

As Al and Mike made their way to their first call of the day, Al explained some of the details of his new job. He explained that Ron was almost as new as Mike and he took over the dog pound from another manager who had just quit one day. The dog pound had more than its share of screw-ups like Stu, who is a great tech but needs to be constantly motivated. He dresses like a pig, works only when he really has to but his parents own a third of all the stock of At Your Service.

There's also Greg who has less than average technical skills, is lazy and is amongst the best dressed in the field. Mike came to learn after awhile the hardest working techs had a tendency to wear dark clothes. The techs who wore light colored clothes were usually afraid to get dirty so didn't. Greg rarely replaced parts and tried to take calls in other territories when his machines needed a lot of work, leaving his backup to maintain his machines for him.

There was Frank, who recently lost his partner in crime Tom. Al explained that Tom was the tech who was taken away by ambulance during Mike's interview. He had the absolute worst attitude of anyone he had ever met, he was let go on the spot after he tried to attack Ron in his office. The ambulance was called after Tom had hurt his back while lunging for Ron. Frank is still here for now only because Ron had to let go of two other guys and reached his limit, they were stuck with Frank for now.

There was the team of Brad and John, two jocks. They grew up together, enlisted in the Marines together, served in Desert storm together and were hired together. Brad was much more technically competent than John and has been seen swapping calls with him. Brad would fix Johns more challenging problems while John did Brad's preventive maintenance or dirty work. Although it's not the preferred way to work, it shows good teamwork and their customers love them both so they're left alone.

Mike asked Al about the fuss over Fusia and Phoenix in the morning meeting. It turns out the accounts are a classic heaven and hell scenario. Fusia is a fashion publication and is famous in the fashion industry; we have two machines there. The place is filled with women, every one of them a perfect ten. When they place a call, every tech wants to get there first.

On the other hand Phoenix is an account that takes recently released criminals who've served their time and teaches them how to operate copiers and work in a mailroom, it prepares them for work on the outside. Many of their students are decent guys but some are very undisciplined and downright scary. No one wants to take Phoenix unless they have to. One of their graduates works at one of our accounts, SafeTnet insurance and is not someone we challenge very often. He's been suspected of breaking the machine to get out of working and is kind of scary looking. No one messes with him including his manager; he seems to get away with anything he wants.

They made their way down the street until they reached a place that looked very run down; the storefront sign read, "Cheap copies-FAST," but had no name. They went through the front door and were met by the manager who greeted them by saying, "Where the hell you been, that piece of crap machine's been down for two days now and who's the fresh meat," referring to Mike.

Al turned to Mike and told him, "This is one of our cesspool accounts," and pointed at the guy who was greeting them, "This is Gil, one of the floaters." Al and Gil had a good laugh while Mike looked around. It was filthy, stuff was piled everywhere, the floors were cluttered with boxes and discarded paper, there was practically no air conditioning and it smelled really bad. Gil was an Asian guy in his fifty's and was lucky if he had three teeth in his head, which probably matched the number of hairs on his head.

They made their way to the copier which had boxes piled up all over it. It had become a shelf while it was down and now needed to be cleaned off.

Al told Gil, "Get this crap off of my machine you turd," again they laughed. Mike told Al he could get use to this and Al replied, "Don't, you need to really know your customers before you can talk to them like this. But it is fun, it beats the hell out of can I help you sir."

It didn't take long before someone came and cleared a space around the copier. As Al and Gil continued to talk, Mike started removing the back covers from the machine. With the covers off of the copier, it took on a rather unfamiliar and rotten odor.

He pushed in the power switch and saw a trace of sparks near the power distribution area.

He opened the door to the power area and was surprised to see two beady eyeballs staring up at him, surrounded by pieces of fur everywhere. Almost by reflex he threw himself back, hitting a wall of empty boxes, some of them came crashing down on top of him.

Al and Gil saw this and ran over to see if he was ok, which he was. Mike told them to look inside the open power distribution area of the machine. Gil looked in first and quickly laughed, then added, "This piece of crap machine is good for something after all, that's the second mouse this thing has caught this year."

Al just laughed it off and Mike got to work with the vacuum cleaner. He also found that a relay board was shorted out and Al showed him how to order a new one. He placed the order and was told where to meet the delivery van that was available.

While Al started doing preventive maintenance, Mike made his way to where he would meet the driver of the delivery van a few blocks away. He waited for a while and saw the van pulling up, it slowed down and a box came flying out of the driver's side window, nearly hitting him in the shoulder. It had the part name he was waiting for and figured it was his part but was shocked at the delivery method, "Airmail?"

He made his way back to the copy center and explained to Al what had happened.

Al informed him that during the interview, Mike had been chosen for the job over a few others. One of the candidates he beat out was the delivery driver's son. The driver has friends in high places so just give it time and hopefully he'll stop after awhile. Al also reasoned that the driver's son must be really incompetent to have not gotten the job, given his dad's contacts. They finished up around lunchtime and Al figured Mike was due for a break.

It was a nice sunny day so he took him to Liberty Square park, he could always find a few of the guys there for lunch and thought it would be a good way to have Mike get used to his new team mates.

Meanwhile, back at the office, Ron had arranged a sit down with Chuck. Ron explained the situation that was unfolding at home in Illinois. He told Chuck, "This move is taking longer than expected; it's really starting to take its toll on my family. My wife is upset we can't sell the house and we don't know when we'll be able to. My daughter misses me and she's crying herself to sleep. She's acting out all day and going into tantrums, she never used to do that. I know I'm just starting out here but they need me back home for awhile. I have to find a way to get my house sold and bring my family out here."

Chuck stared at Ron in disbelief and responded, "If you're asking me if you can leave for awhile the answer is no, absolutely not! You just got here and you're doing a wonderful job with your team Ron. You're just getting a handle on your responsibilities, if you were to leave now you would be starting from scratch all over again. Don't get me wrong, I do feel for you and your family but this is business, you have to find another way! Like I always say, no pain no gain!"

Ron could not believe what he was hearing from Chuck and replied, "You're kidding right, I come to you in good faith, explain to you that my family is falling apart and all you care about is business! If it wasn't for me you'd still be looking for someone to baby sit your little band of misfits and don't think I've forgotten how you played me to get me out here either!"

Chuck looked at Ron and replied, "Look, Ron, Let me see what I can do. Once upon a time the company had a real estate program set up for transfers like yours, maybe there's some remnant of it left. Please understand, I do care about your problem, I just can't let you go right now." Chuck tried to change the subject and asked Ron, "So how's the new kid working out, Mike, he started today, right?"

Ron replied, "Yeah, time will tell. If you don't need me for anything else I need to take care of something."

Chuck responded, "Of course, I'll get on the phone right away with corporate and see about the real estate program."

Ron got back to his office and could feel the frustration building inside him. He wanted to tell Chuck to go to hell and shove the job up his butt however he knew it would probably end his career in New York and Illinois.

He thought to himself, "No pain no gain my ass! No brain, no pain is more like it!"Ron was beginning to understand the man he came to work for and didn't like him much at all. He thought out loud, "No turning back now!

He was finally confident he could straighten out this team of screwballs and was ready to move Angela and Katie out here now. He thought, "It's always something!"

He decided he would spend some company time online looking at real estate agencies in Illinois but could use a bio break first. He opened his office door and overheard Chuck tell his secretary he'd be gone for the day, golfing with a buddy. Ron stepped out into the hallway and let Chuck know he overheard him.

Chuck replied, "I'll get on that real estate problem right away Ron, don't you worry."

Ron muttered under his breath, "You lying sack of crap," and told Chuck, "You have a wonderful day," as sarcastically as he could.

Chuck knew sarcasm when he heard it but just blew it off.

Ron returned from his break, looked out of his window and thought, "I'm really starting to hate this job!"

He grabbed his necktie and started pretending to hang himself when suddenly he noticed a woman looking out of her window across the street from him. She waved and formed her hand into an imaginary gun, held it to her head and pulled the imaginary trigger. She waved at Ron then turned away when someone came into her office. Ron thought to himself, a building buddy, how cool is that.

He took a seat at his desk and started looking for real estate agencies in Illinois finally realizing he was on his own, Chuck would be of no help at all.

Al and Mike headed to Liberty Square park, as they made their way through the lunchtime crowd, Mike took it all in, this was his first job in the city. Before joining the Air Force and going out west, he had worked locally in

Staten Island. The New York crowd was something to behold. There were street performers every few corners, Rolex watches for as low as five bucks and hustlers playing three card monty.

As they got closer to the park they began seeing some of the guys, Al saw Greg in his bright white, never dirty suit and quickly introduced him to Mike. Greg quickly tried to impress himself on Mike by saying stupid stuff like, "Try not to be too intimidated by me, I have a lot of years doing this and you don't but someday you may achieve my level of expertise."

Mike busted out laughing, remembering what Al had told him earlier.

Mike replied, "I think I travel with you next week Greg, they want me to see how not to work." By now a few of the other techs had gathered around and overheard Mike. They started giving him high fives and saying, "Way to go Mike, good one!" Greg just shrugged it off, he was used to it, and the guys were always making fun of him. He had no work ethics and was a horrible guy to have on your team unless you liked doing someone else's job and watching them try to take credit for it.

Mike was then introduced to Brad and John, two techs who were inseparable. John spoke with a heavy

Brooklyn accent and loved to break chops. There were techs from a couple of other teams as well. They gathered around the hot dog stand and shot the breeze. Someone spotted Stu lying on one of the steps and he kind of reminded you of a lizard lying in the sun, unfazed by anything.

Al pointed to a couple of guys and a girl sitting at a table off to the side, they had a tool bag open that looked more like a portable bar. Even from where they were standing Mike could see one of the techs making what appeared to be martinis, the others were playing cards.

Al explained that they were part of the west side team, Bills crew of techs. Al reminded Mike that Bill was the other manager from his interview.

Al added, "They're a better rated team than we are but that's not really saying much. Most of the techs on their team care about the job but those three just don't know how to work."

John replied, "Maybe they do."

Brad added, "Have you noticed, they're always together, I heard they're like a cloning experiment gone wrong."

John replied, "I know someone who worked with them once, he said those three are really weird, probably from family inbreeding or something! You want to laugh, their names are Dave, Daryl and Darla, I hear they're referred to as the smucks."

Al added, "I doubt if it's a coincidence, they've definitely built a reputation. I guess they do their job for the most part but they screw up a lot. They're known to take extended breaks a lot and don't care when they take them. They have a knack for pissing off their customers but somehow make it work. I'm sure they have family somewhere high up in our corporate food chain or fudge their numbers."

Al then explained that the company lived, breathed and died by these monthly spreadsheets the main office kicked out. On them were numbers that reflected everything the techs did each month. They could tell exactly how many hours each tech worked on any machine and how much money was spent on parts each month for every machine in the district. Everything the company did was based on those numbers. Unfortunately a lot of teams learned to manipulate the numbers to the point that it had become a running joke.

They settled into a spot in the park on one of the steps. Liberty Square Park is shaped like an old Roman amphitheatre, basically a series of stone steps, each about a foot deep; each step sank lower and lower until you reached the lowest step and a large square at the bottom. Street performers would put on a free show at the bottom and everyone had a great view.

Someone said, "Mike, check it out, Larry the loser's here," and pointed to a guy on the bottom step. As Mike watched he saw this nerdy looking kid, probably about eighteen years old sitting on the bottom step, he was constantly moving and twisting his head when suddenly he stopped.

John told Mike, "Now watch this."

A rather large woman came up behind Larry and tapped him on his shoulder. Larry turned around and without a word she decked him, I mean one shot on the chin and Larry was out cold. Everyone applauded and Mike wondered if he had missed something. John explained that Larry was a regular at the park and spent his time looking up women's skirts, a real pervert.

Mike and John were sitting next to one another so they started a conversation.

John explained that he lived in Flatbush with his Grandmother.

Mike replied, "I guess you weren't part of the Verrazano bridge migration."

It had long been felt that once the bridge was built between Brooklyn and Staten Island that Brooklyn moved to Staten Island and a good part of Staten Island moved to New Jersey.

John replied, "I could never do that, Brooklyn stays in your blood forever man!"

They continued and John asked Mike where Al had him working at that day. Mike replied, "We just left someplace called the Sloppy Copy shop."

John replied, "We call that place the Sloppy Copy for obvious reasons, the place is a real rats nest."

Mike quickly chimed in, "Literally."

John continued, "People there are upfront and actually easy to please. Don't take Gil too seriously though, he loves to break balls but he's a great guy if you take care of him and especially if you don't try to BS him."

As they were talking, Mike noticed a middle aged woman approach the techs from the west side team. She started yelling at them and Mike could overhear her complaining about her machine being down all morning.

One of the techs replied, "I just fixed your machine yesterday, what do I have to fix it every day. Who the hell sold you that piece of crap anyway?"

The woman replied, "You have to be the worst excuse for service people ever, what's wrong with you guys? Get back to my office and fix that machine!"

She started walking away and Mike heard one of the techs reply, "Hey lady, don't go away mad."

Then the girl named Darla added, "Yeah, just go away!"

Everyone in the area laughed as the woman stood there frustrated.

She then stooped down and picked up something off of the ground.

The three techs started yelling at her, "Don't do it lady, drop it!"

She reared back, threw whatever it was she had picked up then turned and started running. Two of the techs started chasing after her while the other yelled, "You throw like a girl too!"

Mike felt sorry for the woman and asked Al, "Shouldn't we do something, they're not going to hurt her arc thcy."

Al replied, "No, don't worry, their too lazy to chase her far, besides, she'll call the office and Bill will have to deal with them later."

John told Mike, "I don't know how they do it but they rate us worse than them.

Al overheard John and added, "We just suck that bad, at least some of their guy's care about the job, we have maybe three guys who give a crap."

Just then Al got a call from Renee, there was a rush call at the downtown sales office. One of the sales reps had a demo and the copier she needed to show a customer was down. Renee was trying to reach Greg but he was not responding to her call. Al told her that Greg was just with them having lunch at the park, but as usual he was nowhere to be found when you needed him.

Mike shook hands with John, Brad and a couple of the other guys and said he looked forward to working with them.

Al responded quickly, "That won't last long."

As they walked away he heard Brad reply, "But Al, where else can you go for abuse like this!" The other guys made a lot of howling noises as they got further away.

Al added, "They're the biggest bunch of knuckleheads but they are a lot of fun to work with, some of them would help you with anything when they could."

As they made their way through the streets, Mike was pulling Al's tool cart full of tools and realized that even with wheels this thing got heavy after awhile. Twice it almost tipped over when he hit deep cracks in the sidewalk and Al told him to wait for the winter when there's a foot of snow on the ground.

They arrived at the Sales office with an hour to spare before the demo was due to start. The sales rep was at the door as soon as they opened it and was in a panic. Al quickly got to work on the problem. Apparently it was jamming constantly so they tried the usual quick fixes and got nowhere. They examined the area where it seemed to be jamming first and Al saw a sliver of a piece of something shiny hanging inside and removed a large paper clip. The look of relief on the sales rep's face was immediate and she couldn't stop thanking them enough. Al took the moment to introduce Mike to Joyce and asked her to quickly check the machine while there was still time. Joyce made some prints and realized there was a huge black mark where the paper clip had landed and must have damaged the film belt. Joyce again went into a panic and Mike told her not to worry, they would fix it, then looked up at Al and added, "Right Al?"

Al shrugged his shoulders and started pulling the machine apart as Joyce ran to her desk to start her plan B.

With only two minutes to spare Mike and Al were able to replace the damaged film belt and got Joyce to run off a copy. As the print came out, the receptionist paged Joyce over the loud speaker that her two thirty demo had arrived.

You couldn't help but feel for this girl; she was one of the younger sales reps at the company and was just starting out. Unlike the service side of the business where there was camaraderie and teamwork with most teams, sales had a tendency to be more cutthroat. She started heading for the front door and quickly turned back towards Mike and Al, put her hand over her heart and said "Thank you."

Mike drew a blank but remembered coming to with Al's fingers snapping in front of his face and saying, "Snap out of it."

Mike felt an attraction to Joyce right away, why not; she was sweet, sincere and attractive without being overly sexy.

Al laughed and added, "It's your first day Romeo, chill out, wait till you see the girls at Fusia." He explained to Mike that he had seen many office romances go up in flames, leaving problems everywhere for management to cleanup.

Al continued, "Trust me; you don't want to be a part of that, avoid office romances."

As they were leaving, Al made plans to meet Mike at the office in the morning and told him, "Rest up, maybe I can take you to Rosie's tomorrow night." He had overheard one of the guy's talking about Rosie's when he was at the park. He was talking to John at the time so he never asked, but from what he overheard it sounded like fun. Mike waved at Al and said, "I'm going to hold you to that," then headed for the subway. Finally, it was the end of a long day.

The next day Mike made his way to the locker area, where he was supposed to meet Al. As he got closer he noticed most of the techs scrambling away. Renee the dispatcher was up from her desk, which was rare; she saw Mike and quickly approached him. Apparently she was looking for someone to go to Phoenix and wasn't having any luck. Renee approached Mike and started asking him if he was available then quickly answered her own question, "Of course you're not sweetie," she gently patted his face and added, "You're way too green for that place."

Just then Al and Ron came up to them. Al said, "I see you two are getting acquainted." Renee quickly explained to Ron that Phoenix was getting noisy, they had a call the day before but their tech never showed up, now they need the machine for training and it's down, they are desperate.

As they looked around, the locker room was empty.

Renee added, "Don't get me started, a few minutes ago there were at least ten techs over here. As soon as they heard about the call at Phoenix everyone took off!"

Al looked at Ron, Ron looked at Mike, then patted Mike on the back and said, "If you use the bathroom don't go alone. Oh yeah, Al, get Mike the tool number for soap on a rope." Mike quickly realized he was going to Phoenix.

As Mike and Al were at Renee's cubicle he noticed one of the male dispatchers just across from Renee, an older guy. He could not have been too busy as his screen was open to solitaire the whole time Mike was there.

Renee saw Mike looking his way and explained, "That's Dom, he's just waiting for retirement, must be nice. He was here when all this was done by rolodex instead of computers, that's all he does all day."

Al looked at Mike and asked "Are you ready? You have no idea what you're in for." As they were walking away, Mike saw some of the other techs returning to the locker area. John and Brad looked at him and gave him a salute. Another tech made the sign of the cross and John then pointed and laughed.

As they were walking to the site Al explained to Mike what he could expect.

"First, relax; it's really not that bad. Most of the guys are alright but some are a little undisciplined."

As they got closer to the account Mike started to notice a change in the neighborhood. He had been working in office buildings and surrounded by business people. He noticed they were entering a more residential area with brownstone buildings, ornate streetlights and a park across the street. People were reading newspapers and taking their dogs for walks. One woman was walking six dogs and Mike commented, "How could anyone possibly want six dogs to take care of, imagine what her apartment must smell like."

Al replied, "She's probably a pro, some people get paid to watch other peoples dogs." They watched as the dogs became agitated about something and they all started to scatter at once. The poor girl's legs got tied up in the leashes and down she went.

Mike and Al made their way over to help but as they got closer the dogs became increasingly hostile. A little Shih Tzu started snarling and agitated the others. The girl told them to stay back or they would just get worse. She got to the seated position, started untangling herself and thanked them anyway. As they were leaving they overheard her cursing at the Shih Tzu, "Shut up you little runt, you start all the trouble!"

Mike looked at Al and told him "I think I'll keep my day job."

Al replied, "We'll see if you still feel that way after Phoenix."

They rounded a corner and the area completely changed. There was a housing project a block away, a fire hydrant was open and a few kids were running under the spray. You could hear sirens off in the distance and you could see a couple of blocks away there were some prostitutes in the middle of the street. Al explained this was part of an urban improvement zone that wasn't really catching on very well. "If you have to take a call at Phoenix and the hookers are out avoid them, go around the block if you have to but don't go near them. Most of them in this area are on drugs, diseased or psychotic, stay away and never engage them in a conversation."

Mike looked at Al with a smile and replied, "Come on Al, I have a few bucks on me, can't we stop for a little while, huh, can't we," chidingly.

Al looked at Mike with a grin and said, "You're a sicko kid, you'll do well here."

They finally arrived at Phoenix; in front of the building were at least a dozen guys standing around, smoking cigarettes and drinking coffee. The area around the building was fairly clean, but the building itself was rundown and in need of paint. There was a constant flow of cars dropping people off, a couple of the cars were leaving trails of smoke as they pulled away from the building and were extremely noisy.

In front of the entrance was an ornate sign with a large colorful bird rising from flames, smoke and ashes. It was obviously hand carved and beautiful; someone spent a lot of time on it. Al told Mike it was a former student who went on to become a very successful artist.

As they made their way through the entrance it reminded Mike of his old high school during recess, complete chaos!

They met the receptionist, Awilda, a large middle-aged Hispanic woman.
She and Al greeted one another and Al introduced her to Mike.

Awilda welcomed Mike and said, "Ooooh you're cute. I have a niece who would love to meet you sweetie."

She showed Mike a picture of a large, unattractive girl with the hint of a mustache.

Mike replied, "I'm already sort of attached and not able to see anyone else right now, but you're right, she's a hottie."

Awilda laughed then responded, "Al, I like this one, I can tell he has a kind soul." She added, "My niece is so ugly, when she was born the doctor smacked my sister for giving birth to the girl! When my sister was leaving the hospital with her she got a fine for indecent exposure, the girl is ugly. But thanks for not saying anything Mike."

She added, "If anyone here gives you a hard time just let me know, I got your back." She got up, gave Mike a hug and he was almost overwhelmed by the perfume she was wearing. She looked at Al and told him, "Let me get Matt over here for you."

Awilda keyed the microphone, looked at it in a very benign way and yelled, "Matt, get your butt down here."

Mike could hear car alarms going off outside and some of the people in the hallway were holding their ears. With that same benign look Awilda told Al and Mike, "He'll just be a minute, he hates when I use this thing."

Al elbowed Mikes arm and pointed. Matt was at the end of the hallway making his way very quickly to them.

As Matt approached he started unloading his anger on Al right away. "Al, where the hell have you been? That machine's been down all day yesterday. You didn't even call us, I know we're not your favorite customer but we don't deserve this. What the hell am I going to do now? Class is starting and we need that machine."

Al apologized and explained, "We were really backed up and dispatch tried all day to get someone over here but they were unable to."

Mike knew Al was full of crap and imagined himself in Al's position, he wondered how he would handle the situation.

Mike's eyes locked on Matt's cold steely stare, he spit into the wind in a show of complete contempt, but it blew back on to his face. Mike's hands were tied to a pole behind his back and he was facing Matt's firing squad. Matt asked if he had any final words. Mike swallowed hard and replied, "Oh please, please, please, I promise I'll never let you down again, please. I have a family who needs me, what about my sister, she's a virgin, with six kids, what'll they do without me, oh please, please, please, I'll never let it happen again."

Then Mike felt a tap on his shoulder, it was Al asking if he was still with them. Al added, "Let's go to the machine."

As they headed to the machine, Al introduced Matt to Mike.

Matt was middle aged, a little unkempt with a short scraggly beard and well overdue for a haircut. He was one of the first students at Phoenix and had a lot to do with the formation of the copier and mailroom training division. He was an interesting choice for the job considering his background and time served for counterfeiting.

As they made their way down the hallway, Mike glanced into the various rooms along the way. One room appeared to have a mailroom setup, he could see a few guys sorting mail and faxing stuff. Another room had two guys sleeping on a sorting table and someone else was wheeling around the room on a mail-cart.

They passed the men's bathroom and Mike saw someone at the door almost looking like he was guarding it.

They arrived at the copier, which was in a classroom environment and class was in session. The students were seated at their desks and the instructor was writing on the blackboard when Mike and Al entered the room.

Mike heard one student say, "Oh snap, they here," and a couple of other students let out subdued laughs. When the instructor saw them he stopped writing and started in on them right away, just like Matt.

"How can you guys leave me hanging like this, look behind you, do you see this class?" One of the students yelled out, "Yeah bitches," as Mike and Al turned around to see a classroom full of guys staring at them. Most of them looked very angry, but a few probably couldn't care less.

The instructor went on, "How am I supposed to teach them how to run a copier with no copier? Tell me, I'm waiting."

Al responded, "We'll get you running as quickly as possible."

The instructor continued teaching the class as Mike started removing the covers.
He motioned to Al to look, Al rolled his eyes at what they were staring at and it caught the instructor's attention.

The instructor asked Al, "Is there a problem, I'm trying to teach here," with the same nasty attitude. By now even Al was becoming upset with the abuse he was absorbing and finally yelled out, "Yeah we have a problem, who's the knucklehead who spilled coffee into my machine."

The instructor ran over to look and pandemonium broke out. A majority of the students got up and ran to the copier to look, Mike saw at least a half dozen guys leave the room and everyone was yelling over one another.

Finally the instructor's attitude started to change and he became more apologetic.

Al calmed down and told the instructor that this is normally a very expensive, billable call but would see if he could give him a break considering the problem with their response time.

The instructor dismissed his class for the day as Al and Mike inspected the machine. Coffee was everywhere and the machine would require a lot of work.

They made a list of parts they would need and headed for the parts depot.

They arrived at the depot and saw a few tech's standing on a desk, looking out of a large window, one of them had a pair of binoculars.

Al told Mike, "Check this out, look down."

As Mike looked down he could see a rooftop party going on with a pool and garden setup. Some of the women were in lounge chairs around the pool and most were wearing very tiny thongs and bikinis. Mike grabbed the binoculars from one of the other techs and just stared. Another tech grabbed them from Mike and yelled, "Check that one out, double d's at least!"

Mike looked up at Al and told him, "You're going to find me here a lot."

Al replied, "Sicko," and smiled.

It took the better part of the day but they eventually finished repairing the Phoenix machine. The parts they needed weren't expensive so Al told Matt and the instructor he would not charge them this time, a gift for the poor response to their call.

Mike and Al headed to the bathroom to cleanup and Mike noticed the same guy from the morning standing in front of the door. When it became clear they were heading for the bathroom, Mike saw the guy give three taps and a bang with his foot, obviously a warning code. When they got to the door the guy gave a hard stare and Mike almost felt like he needed permission to open the door. Al brushed past the guy and walked through the door. As they walked in, three guys were standing near an open staring at them menacingly.

Mike said, "Hello," to one of the guys who replied, "Yo."

They washed up and got out as quickly as possible.

Al called Ron to let him know how things went at Phoenix, Ron was glad Al had handled things but Al could tell Ron was down about something. He asked Ron how things went with the real estate problem.

Ron replied, "Did you know Chuck is a total butthole?"

Al responded, "Oh yeah, we've all known that for a long time now. Listen, some of us are getting together at Rosie's, why don't you join us, it'll be good to get out of the office for awhile." Ron agreed and told Al he'd start heading over right away.

After hanging up the phone Ron gave it some thought and realized that with all he'd been going through, a bar was probably not the ideal place to be. Still, he felt he had to do something before he lost his mind. He figured, "I'll just stay for a while and drink club soda or something." He looked at the picture of Angela and Katie on his desk, thought about calling them but changed his mind. He reasoned Angela would probably be worried all night if she knew he was going to a bar so he decided not to call them.

As Ron left the office he ran into Chuck at the elevator. Ron asked him if there was any luck with the real estate division.

Chuck replied, "Sorry Ron, I've been very busy lately, in fact you should find the latest numbers for your team on your desk by the morning, I'm afraid they're quite troubling."

Ron was getting close to his breaking point and tried his best not to tell his boss completely off but couldn't hold back any longer.

Ron replied, "You know Chuck, I've been as patient as I can be but I've got to tell you, you're full of crap. Yesterday you told me you would look into it right away and what did you do, you spent the entire afternoon golfing. Today you came in late, grabbed an early lunch and now I'm supposed to believe you've been busy all day!" My family is in crisis and I'm supposed to be concerned about your stupid numbers."

Chuck responded, "You know Ron, as your boss.."

The elevator door opened and Ron left without letting Chuck finish, Ron's response to Chuck was, "Blah Blah Blah, That's all I'm hearing from you right now."

As for Mike and Al, after leaving Phoenix they realized it was four o'clock and they had skipped lunch.

Al told Mike, "Come on, let me buy you a drink."

Mike replied "But Al, I really don't know you that well, what will this do to our professional relationship, will you still respect me in the morning?"

Al replied, "Sicko, let me show you Rosie's, you can usually find a bunch of us their around five o'clock." He added, "Joyce goes there once in awhile."

Mike responded, "Let's go Al, come on, why are you walking so slow?" and looked back at Al with a smile.

Al added, "I invited Ron too, poor guy seems pretty down, he misses his wife and kid a lot. He was planning on their being out here by now, problems moving them from Illinois."

Mike replied, "I know how that feels, when I left for the Air Force it took awhile before I got over missing my family and friends, I can't imagine leaving a wife and daughter, we have to cheer him up some how."

The streets were becoming crowded with rush hour traffic and after an hour of playing pardon me, excuse me with the crowd, they were finally there.

Mike went through the door first and looked around. The bar was in the middle of everything with booths lining every wall and tables everywhere else. They had a small dance floor with a juke box in front of it and a picture of a really hot looking girl in a very skimpy leather cowgirl outfit hanging over the bar. A sign above the picture read, "Don't miss Fridays with Amanda, the Shooter girl."

Mike looked at Al and pointed at the picture.

Al told him, "She's hot, you have to see her, she'll get you drunk and broke in a hurry, the shooters are strong!"

Just then, Ron showed up and they all took seats at the bar, in front of Amanda's picture of course.

The bartender came up to them and asked Al, "I guess you heard, they're looking for a second shooter girl. Are you thinking about the job? You'd look cute in a leather bikini and chaps."

Mike cut in, "Come on Al, I'd do ya."

Ron laughed, looked at Mike and told him, "Holy crap, what have you two been doing all day."

Al added, "You don't know the half of it, Mike, tell him about the sales office and the binoculars."

Mike replied, "I'd rather tell him about the hookers first."

Ron replied, "Oh, we really need to talk, sounds like you had an interesting second day, to think I have to pay you too!"

The bartender looked at Al with a smile and said, "Where do you get these guys from?" The bartender shook hands with Ron and Mike then introduced himself as Bert.

Bert was a thirty something aspiring actor, married with a couple of children. He had always had high hopes of landing a big part in a Broadway play and occasionally would tend bar portraying some character he was auditioning for.

Bert went away for a second and came back with a few beers. Ron looked at the beer in silence for a moment and Bert asked if everything was all right. Ron explained he'd probably just have a club soda. Bert brought Ron a club soda, apologized, then explained, "I should know better than to assume but figured if you're hanging out with this bunch you need to drink, heavily!"

They laughed then sat back and relaxed for awhile, finally!

As Bert worked the bar, Mike looked around and realized there were a couple of waitresses as well. He looked at Al and pointed to one of them, a gorgeous but somewhat stocky girl with long dark hair, sitting in a booth and filing her nails. Al explained that her name was Sandy, lazy as hell and stuck up. He pointed to the other waitress, a short, petite but shapely girl named Robin. He told Mike "Look out for her, she's tough, doesn't take any crap either."

As they were talking, Brad and John came in and sat next to them. John looked at Mike and told him," You're drinking beer after your first call at Phoenix, come on Al, you slippin." Then he looked at Ron, picked up his drink, gave it a whiff and said, "Club soda?"

He waved at Bert and held up five fingers then yelled, "Jacks, Al's buying."

Al quickly replied, "Are you crazy, my wife will shoot me, buying rounds, no way."

The drinks arrived and John noticed there were only four, John asked Bert, "Why you short changing us man?"

Bert replied, "Because one of you isn't a degenerate perv, right Ron."

They laughed and Ron picked up the tab.

John raised his shot glass and said, "To fresh meat," looking at Mike. They all hoisted and downed their shots. Then John added, "Maybe we can finally get rid of that butt hole Greg, what do you say Ron."

Ron replied, "We already got rid of three guys John, someone has to stay and do the work, I have to admit it probably won't be Greg though.

Al started talking about the call at Phoenix, Brad cut in and reminded Ron that Greg was the lead tech at Phoenix, which should explain the no show the day before.

John added, "Who does Greg know, how can he keep doing this crap and getting away with it," as they all turned and looked at Ron.

Ron replied, "Don't look at me, I just got rid of three little retards for you, where the hell was your last boss or even Chuck for that matter?"

Brad raised his glass and proposed a toast, "To our new boss, finally we have a leader!"

They all raised their glasses and said, "To our leader!"

John looked at Brad and added, "Wait Brad, what's that brown crap on your nose, let me wipe that off for you."

They all laughed, including Ron.

Just then, John pointed at the front window and said, "Oh crap, speaking of retards, look who's here!"

They all turned and saw Frank peering through the window, then make his way through the door. Frank came in, approached Ron and said, "Hey Boss, how you doin, I'm glad to see you."

He then pointed at Bert and added, "Yo, my man, get my good friend a drink over here." He pounded the palm of his hand on the bar and added, "C'mon man, I aint got all day, lets go!"

Bert ignored him and Ron added, "Frank, what the hell is your problem, can't you see he's busy?"

Frank replied, "Just taking care of you man, you know I'll always have your back."

John added, "Just watch out for the knife."

Frank flashed John a look and replied, "What, you think you're a tough guy, bad mouthing me, what's your problem man!"

John responded, "Tough enough to beat the snot out of you, bitch!"

Frank replied, "Alright, c'mon outside, you and me right now!"

Ron stood up and told them both, "Alright, both of you calm down. Frank, you need to chill out, we were just sitting here relaxing, why don't you.."

Frank cut him off and replied, "I need to chill out? What about him," and pointed at John. He added, "I see how it is, Johns your boy, alright, I'll remember that!"

Frank turned red and started heading for the door, Ron followed behind him in hopes of calming Frank down. He was hopeful he could develop a rapport with Frank but it was obvious it wasn't going to happen today.

Ron gave up and headed back to the bar.

John added, "You sure you won't take that shot of Jack?"

Ron replied, "No, I'm alright, is it me or does that guy have the social graces of an elephant in a hot tub?"

Al replied, "Good one, that's Frank though, a little rough around the edges."

Brad added, "Watch out for him Ron, he's Toms right hand."

Al added, so where were we, oh yeah, we were talking about Phoenix.

He explained how Awilda tried to set Mike up with her niece.

Mike shuddered and added, "That girl put the ugh in ugly!"

Al replied, "I think Awilda likes you though Mike, she said you have a kind soul."

Mike responded, "I like Awilda but she almost knocked me out with that perfume, smelled like the best you can buy at the dollar store or something. I got a contact high off of that stuff!"

They all laughed then Al continued goofing on the Phoenix instructor's verbal tirade and added, "I so wanted to smack him." With that they all had another good laugh, now that the day was done.

Mike asked the guys, "When I took this job I thought customers would be happy to see us, after all, aren't we like the cavalry coming to the rescue and all? I'm seeing the complete opposite, these people are nuckin futs."

They laughed and Brad said he liked that phrase, "Half of our operators would never know what we were calling them."

Al added, "It's true though, most service related jobs are thankless, people take you for granted."

John chimed in, "I'm probably guilty of that too, a couple of weeks ago I had a plumber fixing my sink, I was so glad to see him leave I forgot to thank him."

Mike added, "See what I mean, the least you could do is tell him what a great job he did or compliment him on his butt crack or something?"

They all cracked up laughing and Al almost choked on his drink but replied, "Mike, your nuckin futs, you're going to fit right in here."

As they were laughing, John pointed to a young couple on the other side of the bar. John told them "Watch this," he had seen them arguing every time the guy's cell phone rang and he picked it up.

The girl told him, "You love that stupid job more than me."

The guy got up to use the bathroom and the girl insisted he leave his phone behind.

He was gone only a minute when the phone rang again.

John said, "Now watch."

The girl picked up the phone and threw it into the guy's beer. Al and the guys started laughing uncontrollably. The girl noticed that they were laughing at her and was embarrassed. She got up off of the bar stool, gave them the finger and stormed out.

John yelled out, "That's not very lady like," just as Robin, one of the waitresses came up behind him. She planted her foot behind his knee and pushed just a little.

John almost went down but caught himself. He turned around and said, "Robin, I should've known, who else."

She cut him off in mid sentence and said, "Dude, you cost me a tip, they were getting my next open table."

Al replied to Robin, "We thought you felt for the girl."

Robin replied, "Hell no! She's a butt hole, she does crap like that every week, always with a different guy too."

Just then, the guy returned and found his phone in his beer.

Mike shouted, "Now that's alcohol abuse," as they turned their heads and laughed.

While John was distracted, Al took ten bucks off of John's money pile on the bar and put it on Robin's serving tray.

Robin winked at Al, started walking away and said, "Thanks John!"
John was wondering why but didn't give it much thought.

They were having such a great time they didn't realize how late it was getting but one by one they eventually left.

Ron was the last to leave and although he had a great night out with his guys, the days frustrations had taken their toll, the beer Bert had brought him was looking pretty good but the shots of Jack Daniels were really hard to pass up, again he thought about Chuck and the conversation they had earlier.

As he walked along the avenue, back to his hotel he passed another bar that had a sign in the window with a dinner menu and realized he hadn't eaten yet. He stepped in and took a seat at the bar. He asked about the dinner menu but the bartender told him the kitchen was closed an hour ago.

Ron replied, "No problem," and without a second thought, ordered a shot of Jack and a beer.

To oblivion and beyond!

Chapter 3 – Up in Smoke

Mike was on the engineering deck with Scotty. The Enterprise was under attack and one of the transducer coils was damaged. Captain Kirk was hailing Scotty for an estimate. Scotty looked at Mike and asked, "How long Mike, we need that coil installed!"

Mike replied, "Should be about ten minutes Commander," as the ship was rocked by a blast and shook violently.

Scotty replied, "My crew is working as fast as they can Captain, plus a wee bit more, it'll be at least another hour."

Scotty put his finger to his lips and said, "Shhhhh laddie, keep this our secret."

Mike got the coil installed in five minutes and Scotty alerted the Captain, "I don't know how, but the coil is operational sir, that's got to be a record."

Just then they heard the photon torpedoes firing followed by a huge explosion.

The Captain hailed Scotty again and said, "Thank your crew for the miracle Commander, the Klingon ship has been destroyed, we are out of danger."

Scotty replied, "Aye Captain."

Scotty looked at Mike and added, "I've been screwing around with the Captain like that for years, how do you think you make Commander laddie?"

Scotty pulled him aside and opened his locker, he told Mike he was saving this for a special occasion and asked if he had ever had some of his Kardashian brandy. It was a little something he picked up on shore leave in the Fernellan system.

He added, "It's known to have a special property that reacts with some species of females, it tends to plump the booty of some lassies."

Just then the Captains really hot blond Yeoman entered engineering and saw the brandy. She asked, "You know I love that stuff Scotty, why are you drinking it without me? "

Scotty looked at Mike then glanced down at her cute plump booty and said, "See what I mean laddie?"

All of a sudden Mike jumped up and was disappointed to hear his alarm clock ringing then thought, "Oh crap, why can't I dream like that every night."

He looked at the time and realized he was running late.

Today was the group meeting uptown and he was supposed to find out where his first territory would be. After a quick shower and even quicker cup of coffee, he was out the door.

It was a beautiful day, perfect for a ferry ride. After a couple of weeks riding the Staten Island ferry to the city, he was starting to enjoy the commute. He got lucky and caught one of the older boats with the wide-open car deck.

He saw his cousin George hanging out towards the back with some of his friends and made his way over there. His cousin was playing pool the night before and was goofing on the guy he beat.

He said, "Hey Mick", which was Mike's nickname to family, "What happened, you sleep in this morning, you got the late boat?" Just then they heard the code and George put out his cigarette. The code was a system that no one can remember starting but was extremely useful if you were a smoker. It was illegal to smoke on the boats but as a cop made his way from one end of the deck to the other, the passengers would let out a quick whistle to alert everyone of his location. Somehow it worked, as long as you were paying attention.

The boat started preparing to dock so everyone braced themselves. Depending on who was piloting and how bad the currents were that day you could really get knocked around if you were standing and not holding on to something.

After docking, he made his way to the crowded, smelly subway. If New York City were to adopt an official odor, it would have to be stale urine.

He arrived at the office with fifteen minutes to spare, said a quick good morning to Gertie and complimented her on the very spring like outfit she was wearing. He thought, "For an older woman, slightly overweight she's kind of sort of hot, kind of."

He caught up with everyone at Renee's cubicle. Al was there and asked Mike, "Are you ready? You get your first territory today."

Mike admitted he was a little nervous but figured he was as ready as he'll ever be.
John overheard Mike and Al then started to break Mike's chops.

"I heard you were getting Phoenix and SafeTnet Mike."
Al replied, "The ex cons all had a vote and demanded you be there technician John, something about making you work late a lot too."

Then Ron made his way into the dispatch area and was walking with a woman no one had seen before. She was tall, had long blond hair she wore in a ponytail and was wearing somewhat loose fitting slacks and a knit shirt. In spite of the loose clothes, you could tell she was muscular under it all.

Ron called everyone into the conference room, some of the guys were already in the room and as usual they were throwing stuff around. As the noise level in the room grew louder, Ron's hangover got the better of him. Out of nowhere Ron screamed out, "All of you shut the hell up already, am I a babysitter or a manager."

He grabbed his head at the place where it hurt the most but it didn't help. The room became very quiet, very quickly as everyone was stunned, Ron had a way of gaining control but it was usually a little less subtle. Even Al was caught by surprise but figured the situation with Ron and his family was catching up with him.

Ron had the new girl sit next to him, for her own safety I guess.

He called the meeting to order and said, "Children, listen up, we have a lot to cover. First, the young lady to my right is Kelly and I don't know who she pissed off but she has been assigned with you guys."

At first the room stayed quiet and Al commented, "Holy crap, I never thought I'd see the day you guys went quiet, twice in one day even.

Ron added, "Don't jinx me Al, quiet is good today, my head is killing me."

Al turned to Kelly and told her, "It's going to be great having you on the team."

Ron added, "Kelly, these children have adopted the name dog pound, welcome to the dog pound."

Then it went back to normal and the guys went back to making barking and howling noises. Kelly looked a little startled but smiled. Mike was close enough to tap her hand to get her attention and told her, "I just started a couple of weeks ago, you should see what they did to me."

With that, a large rolled up ball of paper hit Mike on the head, "That would be about right," Mike told her as he returned fire and laughed.

Ron took control of the meeting again and added, "Mike, I'm glad you're in such a good mood, I don't want you to think I'm throwing you to the wolves, but I'm throwing you to the wolves today."

He handed Mike a list of accounts and said, "Here's your new territory, I had to give you Phoenix and SafeTnet, I hope you don't mind."

Al had a puzzled look on his face until Ron added, "Just kidding."

The room erupted again with a bunch of Ahh's and Ha Hahs from everyone. Ron put his hand to his head again, in pain. Al looked at the group and swiped his hand across his throat in a gesture that said cut it. They responded, realizing Ron was in pain.

Mike commented, "I can't thank you enough Ron, really, I mean it," with a smile so Ron would know he was kidding.

Ron added, "Mike would be getting SafeTnet, but not Phoenix. I'm reserving Phoenix for Brad who will also get Fusia."

Brad was beaming, he had wanted Fusia since he started working at AYS and had an interest in the cute operator there. He had been trying to get closer to her and this would certainly help.

Next, Ron added, "Dress down Friday's will begin this Friday."
Everyone clapped and howled for joy.

Ron quickly added, "It will be a trial for now on a week to week basis. Casual slacks like Dockers, a collared knit or dress shirt and leather lace-able shoes were acceptable. As I said in our last meeting, Sneakers, blue jeans of any color and non collared shirts will get you sent home without pay in a heartbeat."

The room went quiet and everyone looked at Stu.

Stu looked up with a smile and replied, "What?"

Still it was a great deal, it cost a lot to maintain good clothes for a job where you got dirty every day. It only took one week for Mike to tear his first pair of pants. Add to that the fun of wearing a tie when it's a hot, sticky and humid ninety eight degree day in the summer.

Ron kept the meeting going with a lot of the usual stuff. He added, "Clean up after yourselves if you use the lunchroom, don't forget to empty the refrigerator at the end of the week or it would be unplugged. And oh yeah, there's been word from some of the customers that if they need after hours service they could stop in at Rosie's any night of the week, find half of our workforce there and hire a tech."

He added, "I know that's not true, hell I can't even get you guys to work during the day. But just a reminder that it would be considered a conflict of interest and anyone doing so would be fired."

Half the room responded in unison, "Oh crap!"

Ron asked if anyone had anything to discuss and as usual Greg responded.

"I have something, I'm looking at my new territory and noticed it's spread across five blocks, it seems inefficient, can't we change that?"

A few of the guys responded, "Poor Greg."

Ron didn't waste meeting time with Greg and told him he could take it up with him in his office later, "Stop by my office at four thirty if you feel the need." Ron knew he'd never see him so considered it a closed issue.

Ron added, "Alright children, lets get to work, stop at Renee's cubicle on the way out and see what's hot, I don't mean the dispatcher's either."

As they made their way out of the meeting, Al explained Mike's new territory to him. He told Mike that Ron was starting him off light, but half of the machines used to belong to Greg, which meant they needed a lot of work. If he needed help just call on Brad, John or himself. His parts locker was behind Active Graphics, one of the copy centers he picked up.

They got to Renee's desk and Renee was waiting for Mike.

She said, "Ok stud, I hear your all mine now, you ready for me?"

Mike replied, "Well, I usually like to get to know a girl first but alright, I have to admit you're a hottie Renee. Can we go somewhere a little more private though?"

Al laughed and Renee responded, "Were going to get along just fine wise-ass," she added, "You just happen to have a call at Active Graphics."

Al reminded Mike it was the place where he was going to keep his parts, the perfect first call. Mike grabbed his tool cart from the locker room and made his way to the elevator. He was thrilled to be taking his own calls and thought, "Finally!"

When he got to the elevator another tech was there waiting with his tool cart. He had it loaded with parts, two tool bags and a small license plate that read, "I brake for no one."

Mike asked him, "You have a license and registration for that thing?" and smiled.
Mike introduced himself and explained it was his first day with his tool bag.

The other tech introduced himself as Julio and explained, "My territory is really widespread, it's a pain in the butt running for parts all the time so I carry as much as I can."

The elevator door opened and Julio got on first, you could tell he was used to maneuvering his cart, he did a complete turn on one wheel and backed it right in.

Mike fumbled through and Julio held the door open for what seemed forever.

Julio laughed and said, "You flunked the road test rookie but give it time, when you can make it through Wall Street during lunchtime without running anybody over you pass."

While Mike headed to his first call, Ron sat at his desk, head still pounding from his hangover and he wondered what to do next. He spoke to his wife earlier and there was no improvement at home. He didn't dare tell her that he started drinking again, she was suffering enough already. He had been staring all morning at the spreadsheet Chuck had left him but having problems concentrating. He did find one number that stood out, somehow his group had been using parts at a phenomenal rate before he took them over. Considering this group's reputation it was extremely odd.

Ron's door was open just a crack and he could hear Millie pounding away at her typewriter. Each stroke she made sounded like thunder going off in his head, it was excruciating. He got up to close the door just as Al knocked and entered.

Ron had just circled the unusual number so he asked Al about the data. Al admitted he was at a loss and added, "Most of these knuckleheads should get an award for using the least amount of parts."

Ron smiled and put down his pen.

Al asked, "Are you alright Ron, you seemed really stressed during the meeting, how's the headache?"

Ron admitted he had no idea what he was going to do next. The situation at home wasn't improving and he had to get back somehow. Chuck was being a complete butt-hole about the whole thing. Ron confided to Al that he may have to quit, he was feeling trapped but his family would come first, job or no job.

Just then the door opened and Chuck barged in.

Ron told Chuck, "Don't you ever knock? You know I sometimes take a break around this time of day, I turn off the lights, turn the music on low and pleasure myself, you don't really want to walk in on that do you?"

Al could hardly contain himself and almost busted out laughing.

Chuck just ignored them both and asked about the spreadsheet, Al excused himself and told Ron he had to help John with a problem he was working on, he walked out, grinning from ear to ear.

After Al left, Ron stared at Chuck for a moment in silence. Ron finally spoke up and told Chuck, "You really need to let me go home for awhile Chuck, please don't force me to make a choice between you and my family."

Chuck replied, "I know you don't believe me Ron but I really am trying to pull some strings with corporate. You need to know however that I can't afford to let you go right now. If you were to leave I couldn't guarantee your job will be here when you get back. If you leave on bad terms the company in Illinois won't accept you either. Please be patient Ron and don't do anything foolish."

Ron felt an anger stirring inside that he had never felt before, ever. Still he reasoned that it would be a mistake to act on that rage right now, he would probably do something he would regret and end up in jail. He briefly pictured himself with his hands wrapped around Chuck's throat.

Without a word, Ron got up and left with Chuck tagging along behind him. Chuck kept repeating over and over, "Ron, don't do something you'll regret later, stop and think for a moment. Like I always say.."

Ron cut him off and replied, "What Chuck, what do always say. That you have no idea what you're doing, that you're a lying sack of crap." When Ron got to the elevator he turned and added, "Chuck, you're the most heartless, pathetic, lying little excuse for a man I've ever met."

The elevator door opened and stopped Ron's verbal assault, he got on the elevator, smiled as the door was closing and gave Chuck the finger. The look on Chuck's face was priceless and although slight, Ron finally felt some relief. However, the anger and frustration had taken its toll on Ron and he was now feeling an overwhelming desire to drink again.

Mike made it to Active Graphics, met the operator Dave and introduced himself as their new tech. Dave asked about Greg not being their tech anymore. Mike responded diplomatically that Greg was needed elsewhere and he would do his best to take care of their needs from now on. Mike couldn't tell Dave the truth that Greg was a horrible tech, had no work ethics and was routinely shifted around before he completely ruined the machines.

Mike got right to work and asked Dave what the problem was. Dave explained that the copies were coming out dirty so Mike started inspecting the machine. He noticed that a piece of paper had gotten into a cleaning unit so he pulled it apart and realized it needed a cleaning brush. Mike asked Dave if he could check Greg's parts in the back, grabbed the keys and went around the block to the side entrance. He opened the outside door that led into a long, dimly lit brick hallway. As he got closer to the second door he started to smell an extremely pungent odor, when he got to the door he looked to his left and was startled to see someone standing there, smoking a joint.

The man exhaled just as Mike spotted him and said, "Relax man, it be cool." He put out his hand and added, "I'm Roger, I work in the building."

Mike shook his hand, coughed and replied, "Glad to meet you Roger."

Roger offered him a hit off of his joint and Mike replied, "Not right now, I'm working."

They carried on a conversation for a good ten minutes. Roger explained he was a messenger in the building and took his breaks in the hallway. He was from Jamaica, which explained the dreadlocks that were partially covered by the yellow, green and black wool pullover hat.

Roger told Mike, "I see a lot of techs go in and out of here, they always be stressing so." He took another hit off of his joint and added, "Trust me," then released the smoke into Mike's face and continued in a strained voice, "Don't be stressing so, dem fat cats make all the money and we be dying young." He made a weird noise like he was sucking his teeth and continued, "Relax, enjoy the day God give you."

By now Mike was almost feeling a contact buzz. He replied, "I know what you mean," and kept talking as he went into the parts room, got the part and came back out.

Roger just looked at him and added, "See what I mean boy, you be stressing so. Don't worry, I'll school ya."

Mike shook hands again and replied, "I know your right but I really have to go, it was great meeting you Roger."

When he got back to the copy center Dave said, "I can smell, I mean, tell you met Roger and added, "Whew," then waved his hand like he was clearing the air. "Don't mind him, he's a pretty decent guy, I hear he was a high-ranking administrator somewhere but got tired of it all and just quit one day."

Just as Mike was finishing up he received a call from Renee. "The calls are backing up, are you done with Active yet?" she asked. Renee sounded surprised to hear he was finishing up and added, "That's my boy," when Mike said he could take another call.

She explained that John's territory was backing up and he could use a hand, there was a call in one of his copy shops in the village he couldn't get to. The name of the account was Nature's copy and it was a true Mom and Pop shop or family owned business. Renee dispatched him on the spot and after a half hour walk he arrived.

Mike opened the door and triggered the wind chimes that served as a doorbell. A slender woman who was probably in her sixties came out from behind a beaded curtain and welcomed Mike. The shop was dimly lit, mostly sunlight and scented candles illuminated the room. Mike noticed the lights were off and the woman who introduced herself as Bernice explained that they used as little electricity as possible, "We have to take care of Mother Earth you know."

She looked at Mike, put both of her hands up to his head and told him, "You have the most beautiful aura." Bernice was close enough for Mike to tell she had been smoking some of Roger's weed.

Just then, a very large, long haired man came out from behind the beaded curtain and yelled at Mike, "Hey man, get the hell away from my wife." Then added, "Just kidding dude, you can have her, so long as you take the baggage too. Hey Bernie, how many kids are we up to?"

Bernice replied, "Oh Arthur," she looked at Mike and added, "Don't mind him, he's such a stoner." Apparently they were both stuck in the nineteen sixties and Arthur was a dead ringer for an aged Tommy Chong from the Cheech and Chong movies Mike had loved so much. Although they were a little flaky, he immediately took a liking to them.

Mike asked Bernice, "So what seems to be the problem today?"

Bernice replied, "I try to turn it on and nothing happens."

Arthur chuckled, "She gets that a lot dude, believe me." He rolled his eyes and added, "Do you have any girl friends you wanna swap?"

Bernice continued, "Arthur, stop that," and added, "It just doesn't work anymore." She looked over at Arthur and added, "The copier either."

Mike almost busted out laughing but contained himself and replied, "Let me take a look at the machine," and started unpacking his tool cart.

He started taking off the back covers and saw a framed photo on the wall of a much younger Arthur and Bernice at what looked like Woodstock. There was another photo of them at a Grateful dead concert with a caption that read, "We love dead people."

Mike started troubleshooting and checked the wall power, then realized there was no power feeding the machine. He asked where he could find the circuit breaker and found no power there either. He called Arthur over to show him and Arthur just stared in disbelief.

He told Mike, "You gotta do something man, we need this machine running today. I finally got a new customer, I don't wanna piss him off."

Bernice overheard, she approached them and asked, "What's wrong boys?"

Mike replied, "I hate to burst your bubble but I think you need an electrician or Con Ed, you have no power." Mike went to the light switch and tried to turn on a light, nothing happened.

Bernice looked at Mike, gave the cutest chuckle and replied, "Oh wow, I don't believe I did that, I knew I forgot something." She went to her desk, pulled out her Zodiac chart and turned it over, it was the electric bill.

Arthur told her, "Aw Bernie man, how can you do that, and you call me a stoner."

Bernie ran to the phone and started calling Con Ed.

Arthur started asking Mike, "Dude, so long as you're here, look at this new paper I need to run. Do you think the machine can handle it?" He held up a sheet of paper with a lot of dots and bumps on it.

Mike asked, "What's up with the bumps?"

Arthur replied, "They're seeds dude, were gonna get everyone to start running this stuff. In ten years every landfill will be growing pot, it's awesome! I thought of it myself, do you think they'll let me patent it man."

Mike shook his head and replied, "I don't think it'll ever get through the machine Artie but you might make a fortune with it on EBay; just don't get caught."
Artie replied, "What bay? You mean the harbor, right dude?"

Mike wished them luck with their power issues, told them how much he enjoyed meeting them and started heading to his parts locker.

Along the way, Renee called Mike again and advised him that he had another call, this one was at another of his new accounts, Exporters ltd.

He feedback and closed the call from Nature's copy with Renee on the spot and started heading to his next call at another new account, Exporters ltd.

Upon arrival he was introduced to the operator Daryl who explained his machine was jamming. Mike was able to fix it quickly but realized the machine was neglected badly and needed a lot of work. He ordered the parts for next day delivery and finished up for the day thinking to himself, "Not bad for the first day!"

The next day started with a call from Renee. Mike picked up the call and said, "Hi Renee, I'm flattered that you keep calling me like this but people are going to start talking."

Mike was going to say more but Renee could be heard laughing on the other end, then cut in, "Yeah, yeah, yeah wiseass, you ready for another call?"

Mike explained that he planned on going back to Exporters that morning to rebuild their machine but they were able to print. He was already learning that customers could put up with almost anything, flames could be shooting out of the back of the equipment, so long as they were able to print they could care less.

Mike could hear Al in the background asking Renee if the machine was at least running, she responded, "Yeah."

Renee relayed to Mike, "Overtime could be approved for Exporters if needed but SafeTnet is down and we need you there this morning."

Mike replied, "No problem, I'm on my way."

As he hung up the phone Mike realized he was going to meet Carl, the operator who graduated from Phoenix. He had a reputation for being mean, ornery and breaking his machine a lot.

Mike called SafeTnet and asked for Carl. The guy on the other end had a deep, gravelly voice and responded, "This is Carl, who's this," with attitude.

Mike replied, "This is Mike, one of the techs from At your service. I heard you had a problem with the machine. I'm on my way."

Mike would normally ask some questions but the way Carl sounded he thought a short and sweet introduction would work best.

Carl responded, "So, just get over here and fix this thing, piece of crap machine" and hung up.

Mike thought out loud, "That went well."

Back at the office, Al and Renee were wondering where Ron was; he usually arrived at work early but was nowhere to be found this morning. They tried calling his cell phone and hotel room but Ron never picked up.

At the hotel, Ron was just waking up, unaware of what had happened the night before until he tried to get out

95

of bed. The awful throbbing pain in his head and what had to be the worst case of cottonmouth reminded him quickly. He slowly moved to the seated position and felt his stomach churn, then tighten up. He made his way to the bathroom and slipped on an empty bottle of Jack Daniels that was lying on the floor. He crawled to the toilet and threw up violently. After what seemed like an eternity, he was finally able to stand up. Along the way he caught a glimpse of himself in the mirror and had to do a double take, he looked horrible. His eyes were bloodshot and as he turned his head he saw what looked like a skid mark on his right cheek. As he tried to rub it off it looked like asphalt or something. He made his way back into the bedroom and saw the remains of a second bottle of Jack Daniels on his dresser. He again looked in the mirror and thought to himself, "What the hell did I do!"

Then he thought about Angela and Katie and how he let them down, "How could I be so stupid, why didn't I just stay home."

He looked at the time, twenty after ten and thought out loud," I better get my ass to work."

He looked at the remains of the bottle of Jack on his dresser and realized it was still half full. Without a second thought he picked it up and chugged half of it, crawled back into bed and said, "Screw it!"

As for Mike, after twenty minutes of fighting his way through rush hour crowds, he arrived at SafeTnet, took a deep breath and walked into the copy center.

There was a short dividing wall about three feet high blocking access to the production area and one of those bells you tap to get the operators attention. Mike tapped it once but somehow got two rings out of it.

Suddenly a huge man, black, probably in his upper fifty's and at least six feet tall came out from behind a curtain where he had a collating counter he was working at.

He said, "You know I'm not deaf, one ring is enough, damn bell."

Mike introduced himself as his new tech and put his hand out. Carl looked at it for a second, paused then shook Mike's hand.

Carl's hand was huge and powerful, with no effort Carl was hurting Mike's hand.

Carl quickly explained, "This machine's broken every day. I call Greg, he comes in and the next day it's the same crap all over again."

Mike replied, "Let me see what I can do."

Carl responded, "Even Greg said it's a lemon, damn piece of crap."

Mike asked what the problem was today and started looking for the cause. As he pulled off the covers he could see the machine was a train wreck, most of the chains were rusting and everything was filthy.

The main problem today was a broken clutch on the main paper feeder. Replacing the clutch was a two-man job. He ordered the part and was told the delivery van could be there in an hour. He was to meet Sam the delivery guy on the street.

Mike thought, "Great, maybe I should go get a football helmet."

He then contacted Renee and explained that he would need help removing the paper feeder, she replied, "Start doing what you can, I'll get someone over there."

He started vacuuming the machine and noticed Carl working with his collator. Most of these machines today were plastic and he wondered if Carl's reputation for intentionally breaking stuff wasn't ill conceived, his hands were huge, everything he worked with was like a toy.

Anyway, the machine looked worse and worse the more he looked. He was able to remove the paper feeder on his own but had to leave it on the floor. He went out to the street and waited for the delivery van, which showed up right on time. As expected, Mike watched the part come flying out of the window, just missing him and the van continued on.

Mike yelled out, "Thank you, douche bag!"

Mike heard laughter behind him and turned around. It was Kelly, the new girl and Greg.

Kelly asked, "What's up with the special delivery."

Greg added, "What did you do to piss Sam off like that?"

He looked at Greg and replied, "I guess some people just know how to work Greg," with a slight tone of sarcasm. The comment went right over Greg's head, but Kelly knew it was directed at him and said, "Ouch!"

Kelly was already advised about Greg, everyone was.

They started walking towards SafeTnet and Mike asked Kelly, "Why are you traveling with Greg today?"

She replied, "Al is stuck in the office, something about Ron being out today so Al asked me to travel with him. He explained I should observe how he works and don't do anything he does."

Mike laughed, "That's an oxymoron, you can't observe how someone works if they never work."

They arrived at SafeTnet and Mike got the parts installed on the main paper feeder. Greg tried impressing Kelly by showing her the machine and told her, "Look how clean I kept this machine." Kelly noticed the vacuum on the floor, the mess around the machine and replied, "Why do I get the feeling Mike had more to do with that than you did."

They overheard Carl give a loud laugh from behind the curtain.

As Greg looked around the machine he pointed out some of what Mike had already observed. Rusted chains, worn parts and tried to degrade Mike in front of Kelly by saying, "Mike, I know your new but you really can't let your machines go like this, I can make a list of worn parts a mile long and."

Mike cut him off and replied, "Save it Greg. I made a list of all the parts you never ordered while this account was yours and I plan on putting them in when I can."

Again they heard Carl give a chuckle; his voice was so deep you couldn't miss it.

Kelly excused herself to use the restroom and Mike started prepping the machine to reinstall the paper feeder. Greg was being useless as usual, Mike asked for his help but Greg replied, "I'd love to help you more but I'm wearing this clean suit plus I'm tied to this boat anchor today," meaning Kelly. He added, "I have an image to maintain you know."

Greg didn't realize it but Kelly had just returned and was standing right behind him when he made the rude comment. Without saying a word, Kelly picked the paper feeder up off the floor and placed it on top of the machine, normally a struggle for two people, she did it with ease.

Mike smiled as Kelly gave him a wink, she then turned her eyes on Greg, who had finally shut up and they heard Carl laughing in the background again.

They gave up on Greg so Mike and Kelly installed the parts themselves as Greg kept dusting off his white suit. They finished up and got the machine running again, Mike told Carl he had ordered parts and would return sometime next week to install them. He further explained to Carl, "In spite of what you were told, the machine's not a lemon. I can see it needs a lot of work, but I promise I can improve its performance."

Mike thought he saw a smile on Carl's face and told him, "Next I'll fix that freaking bell for you," and left.

Mike and Kelly were thinking about a late lunch when he got a call from Renee.

Exporters called and said the parts were in but the machine went down again.

Mike apologized to Kelly and told Renee he would be right over.

Kelly looked at Greg and asked, "Can we go too."

Greg responded, "It's getting late, we shouldn't get tied up."

Mike was getting tired of being nice to Greg and finally blew off a little steam.

Mike replied, "How can you be so lazy Greg? It's only two o'clock and you're ending your day already. Do you realize all the work you left me with in your old territory? You have to be the worst guy I ever tried to work with. What the hell is wrong with you?"

Greg kept quiet as Mike walked away.

Mike told Kelly, "I loved working with you though Kelly."

He had a part to pick up at Active Graphics before heading to Exporters so he bought a knish and bottle of water from a street vendor then headed to his parts area. He saw his new Rasta friend Roger hanging out, smoking a doobie as usual and thought again, "Some people really do know how to live."

He said, "Hey Roger, how they hanging today," while trying to be upbeat.

Roger replied, "I see you not stressing so much today."

Mike responded, "Actually, I am having a bad day today," and explained some of the details.

Roger reached into his shirt pocket and pulled out another joint, then added, "Mike, I been saving this one just for you man, what you say."

Mike looked at his watch and thought about it, by the time he got to Exporters they'd be closing, the operator said he would have to work alone anyway.

Mike replied, "Why not? What could go wrong? Fire it up!"

As they were passing it back and forth, Roger explained Greg to Mike. He had been observing Greg for quite some time and told Mike, "Greg may have it right you know, like I tell you man, the rich fat cats make you work harder and harder. For what, so dey get more and more rich and you be stressing so," then he made that weird sucking noise with his teeth again.

By now, Mike was feeling pretty relaxed and told Roger, "This is some good stuff. Where did you get this from?"

Roger replied, "Me Grandmother sends it from the old country, she grows it herself."

Mike was in the middle of inhaling and almost choked with laughter.

They both laughed for a while about anything and everything. Then Mike looked at his watch.

He said, "Roger, thank you man, I feel so much better now, but I really have to get going."

Roger told Mike he'd always keep one on the side for him. They shook hands, Roger gave Mike a hug and told him, "Stay cool man, don't work too hard tonight."

Mike laughed and told Roger, "I think you took care of that for me, thanks Roger. " Mike grabbed the part he needed and took off.

He arrived at Exporters just around four o'clock. Daryl was getting ready to leave and asked Mike if he wanted him to leave the radio on. At the moment it sounded pretty good.

Mike was feeling awesome and went about his work as relaxed as he had never felt before. After cleaning the machine and getting the parts installed, it was just a matter of calibrating everything. All the hard stuff was out of the way and he was starting to get really comfortable, his feet were sore so he took off his shoes. He found himself moving more and more to the music. Then some vintage Foghat came on the radio and he started singing to the song, "Slow ride." "Slow down, take it easy," the song went on.

"Yeah," he thought, "This is cool."

All of a sudden, out of nowhere he heard a voice from behind him say, "Are you alright in here?"

Mike turned around to find Ted, the owner of the business watching him and thought, "Oh crap!"

Ted came in and sat down at Daryl's desk. He started asking questions like, "What the hell is wrong with this machine? Do these machines have a life span? It seems to have a lot of issues lately, do I need a replacement?"

Mike was caught completely by surprise and was totally unprepared for the onslaught.

He responded, "I'm Mike," and put his hand out.

Ted shook Mikes hand and said, "That's nice, but what about this machine? It's at the end of its life, isn't it!"

The best response Mike could come up with was, "I'm your new Ted tech, I mean tech, Ted."

Then, all of a sudden words that made sense started coming out of nowhere.

Mike added, "I'm actually here addressing those questions right now. I was here yesterday and noticed the machine needed work, I'm here installing the parts tonight so I wouldn't interfere with your daytime production. Looks like one of the parts didn't quite make it through the day. I tried but you know what they say, best made plans."

Mike realized he was starting to babble so he shut up, hoped for the best and waited for Ted's response.

Ted looked down at Mike's feet, which had no shoes on them and replied, "Well," then paused and added, "I appreciate the effort, it's more than that jerk Greg ever did.

By the way, I'm glad you know how to enjoy your work. I too sometimes kick the shoes off and blare the stereo when I'm here late."

Mike looked down and noticed that Ted wasn't wearing any shoes either.

Ted asked Mike if he could do him a favor and check his office printer. Although he wasn't required to check it for him, Mike figured it would be a good time to score some points with Ted.

Mike found a loose cable and took care of it for him, then realized Ted had some old Chuck Berry music playing and complimented him on his choice.

Mike went back to work, finished up and got out as quickly as he could realizing he had just dodged a bullet.

"Holy crap," he thought, "I can't believe I just did that."

He swore he would never indulge himself again while working. Roger would have to de-stress without him.

As for Rogers's thoughts about Greg, Mike saw two of Greg's customers turn today. They were upset when he walked in, a little happier when he left and thought,

"I think I'll stick with my way," which was actually Al's way.

It was late, he was tired so he started heading for the subway.

He suddenly remembered his dream from the other morning.

He looked up and thought, "Beam me up Scotty, and crack a bottle of that Brandy while you're at it."

Chapter 4 – It Can Work, If You Work It

Chuck arrived at the office, it was ten in the morning and he noticed that Ron's office door was still closed. He opened it, walked in and realized Ron was not there yet. It had been two days and Ron was nowhere to be found. He recalled their last conversation and the incident in the elevator then realized he had probably lost his best shot at fixing his crew of misfits. He thought, "Ron must have returned to Illinois, let me call his home."

He asked Millie to call Ron's home in Illinois and transfer the call into his office when she got Ron or his wife on the line.

Chuck watched as Millie opened her Rolodex, found his card and started dialing her rotary phone.

Chuck shook his head and thought, "She's got to be the slowest secretary in New York," then went inside and waited.

Angela picked up on the first ring, hoping it was Ron. She explained that she hadn't heard from Ron either, not for a couple of days. She added, "The last time I spoke to Ron he was very upset, something about his boss being the most inconsiderate man he ever met!" Then added, "Mind you I'm cleaning up the language for you."

Angela heard silence on the other end, she added, "Chuck, are you there?" but still no response so she hung up.

In spite of Chuck's position in management he was actually a very timid, non-confrontational man. Angela and Ron had it right however, he was always very self centered and inconsiderate. He knew he was being unreasonable with Ron but he was truly desperate for someone to straighten out the dog pound, he knew he never could.

After hanging up the phone, Angela imagined the worst. She could tell Ron was coming unglued, he had made only one meeting the entire time he was in New York and he hated the meeting. He stepped into a situation in New York that seemed impossible to deal with. Add to that the problems in Illinois, the fact that he missed herself and Katie, it was all a disaster waiting to happen.

She broke into tears as she thought about her husband, all alone in a place like New York, probably drinking again.

Angela recalled how Ron was always her rock, during their High School day's when they first started dating, she was a cheerleader and Ron was on the football team. The cheerleading captain Janet, was dating Ron's quarterback and always had it in for them.

She remembered the day that Janet and her minions stuffed her locker with tampons, talk about embarrassing! She opened the locker and they just fell out all over her, the entire school laughed at her for a week.

But Ron got even with them for her, he snuck back into school later that night and stuffed Janet's locker with the same tampons, only dipped in ketchup.

In spite of her tears she couldn't help but smile as she remembered the look on Janet's face when she opened the locker, she was screaming in shock, "Gross!"

The quarterback didn't throw a pass to Ron for the next two games and they lost both games. The coach finally had to step in and tell the quarterback to knock it off or he'd be kicked off of the team. The coach knew Ron was the go to guy, the guy who could make a difference, a winner.

She burst into tears again as she thought about her man, what could she do, New York was so far away.

She remembered the old Ron before his heavy drinking started. He had always found a way to get what he wanted. Back in college when they were separated by four hundred miles, Ron drove all the way to her school one night on the anniversary of the day they met. He bribed her roommate and spent the night in her dorm, then drove all the way back to his school to take his final exam, on very little sleep.

They had the perfect life; they loved each other deeply and were absolute best friends. After getting married and having Katie, Ron was promoted to manager, they bought their house and it was all like a dream come true.

Then Ron's mother died a painful death to cancer. A few months later, he and Angela had their second child, a son who unfortunately died a month after birth, they were crushed.

It was then that Ron started drinking heavily. Angela still loved him and understood his pain but couldn't help but be resentful, she was hurting too. When she needed him most he wasn't there for her.

It slowly began to eat away at their marriage; Ron was coming home later and later, drunk and reeking of alcohol. It wasn't until she threatened to throw him out for fear of her and Katie's safety that Ron began to understand.

Ron struggled hard to get sober and became very involved with Alcoholics Anonymous. Finally after a year, sobriety took root and her man was back.

She knew she had to do something, Ron needed her and she had to get to New York, now!

But what about Katie, she could leave her with her Grandparent's but Katie already missed Ron, she'd be devastated if her Mom was gone too, what to do?

She fought through the tears and reasoned that somehow Katie would have to come along. She got on the phone and called her babysitter Jane, who agreed to join her on a trip to New York. Angela booked the next flight out and they were on their way.

They arrived at the hotel around midnight, poor Katie was so tired she woke up once in a while but in a daze. They got to their room, put Katie to bed and Angela prepared for the worse. She booked her room a few floors below Ron's, not knowing how bad Ron would be. Angela did not want to expose Katie to any more of this than she had to, not that Ron was ever a mean or nasty drunk.

She kissed Katie good night, looked into Jane's eyes and said, "Wish me luck," as the tears began to well up in her eyes again. Jane gave her a hug and replied, "Ron's a good guy Angela, I'm sure it's gonna work out. Go and don't worry about Katie, I'll take good care of her, you go get your man."

Angela arrived at Ron's door, she could hear loud music playing inside and thought, "Please be alone in there Ron, please be alone." She thought to herself, "I can handle a lot of things but another woman is above and beyond."

Still she reasoned he would never do that.

She wiped away the remains of her tears, braced herself, and then knocked on the door. Angela heard Ron yell out, "Alright already, I'll turn the music down."

She knocked again, heard the door unlock and then open.

Without looking, Ron started to say, "I told you I'd turn the music." but stopped when he realized who it was.

He stopped in mid sentence and had the dumbest look on his face, then added,

"Angie, I'm so glad to see you baby, c'mon in, have a drink, c'mon."

Angela wrapped her arms around him and burst into tears.

She told him, "I'm so glad you're alright, I've been so worried about you!"

Ron replied, "Worried, about me?"

He was slurring his speech and all Angela could hear was, "Wurrout me."

She responded, "I see you have your old friend in here keeping you company, what happened?"

Ron put the dumb look back on his face again and really didn't know what Angela was talking about but then replied, "What would my cousin Ray be doing here?" and made a loud belch, then added, "Scuse me," and hiccupped.

She grinned and told him, "Oh honey, we have a lot of work to do, don't we?" Angela entered the room and realized that housekeeping hadn't been there for at least a few days. It looked like Ron's hygiene took a beating as well, he had a two day old five o'clock shadow and needed a shower badly.

They talked for at least an hour, Ron was so happy to hear Katie was there he couldn't wait till morning. Angie convinced him to shower and shave before going to bed so he could see her first thing in the morning but it was really because he just reeked.

The following morning, Ron opened his eyes and felt the awful hangover he was growing accustomed to waking up with. He sat up, planted his feet on the floor and was preparing to stand up when he felt something move behind him, on his bed. He then heard a feminine sigh and sprang up, so fast he immediately felt a throbbing in his head and exclaimed, "Owww!"

He turned around and was in shock when he saw the form of a woman under the covers, not remembering that Angela had arrived the night before. Ron immediately panicked and started pacing the floor. He was babbling on and on, "Oh no, what did I do, how could I be so stupid!"

He gently sat back down on the bed and tried pulling back the blanket that was covering his mystery guest's face.

She sighed again, Ron panicked, turned too quickly and flipped off of the bed. He sat on the floor, rubbing his head and heard the woman call his name. He was puzzled, the voice sounded just like Angela's. He slowly lifted himself and peered over the top of the mattress until.

"Angie," he exclaimed, "It's you!"

He jumped on top of her and let out a loud scream for joy. By now Angie was wide awake and wondering what had gotten into Ron.

He explained, "Baby, I had no idea, when did you get here, was I asleep when you arrived?"

Angela replied, "Honey, don't you remember, you were wide awake when I got here, very lit but wide awake."

Then Angela realized that he would never have remembered that Katie was here as well. She added,

"Honey, why don't you and I shower and get ready for breakfast, I have another surprise for you.

Ron was smiling from ear to ear and Angela realized that he had misinterpreted her meaning.

She thought to herself, "Oh well, it's been a few weeks, I give him five minutes and he'll be done, but tonight his ass is all mine!"

She grabbed his hand and they ran into the shower.

Back at the office, Al and Chuck were gathered around Ron's desk trying to figure out what they were going to do next.

Chuck told Al, "This is the third morning now, if he's not in Illinois where could he be?"

Al replied, "The guy's really miss him, at least the one's who do any work. The other ones are jumping for joy, they're starting to revert back to their old ways. Renee told me Frank doesn't return her calls and Greg, well, Greg is still Greg."

Just then, Bill knocked on the door, which was open and asked if he could join the party. Al and Chuck just looked at him and Bill added, "Still no sign of Ron?"

Al replied, "I'm afraid not."

Bill responded, "Have you called the police yet,? I've only known Ron a short time but I can tell he's a stand up guy, if he's not coming to work then something's wrong.

Al and Chuck looked at each other, Bill caught the look and asked, "What?"

Chuck replied, "I haven't called the police yet only because they require twenty four hours before you can file a missing person's claim."

Al added, "That's passed, we can call now!"

Bill asked Chuck, "Is there any reason you can think of for him not to show up?"

Al replied, "You bet your ass there is!"

Chuck looked up at both of them and replied, "You think this is easy, running this place.

Al didn't let him finish and added, "You think this has been easy for Ron, he needs his family, don't you get it Chuck, he can't function like this. You've been looking for someone to straighten out these knuckleheads, well he was here. I'm telling you Ron was your man Chuck, but you blew it. You should've kissed his ass, instead you crapped all over him. I don't blame him if he never comes back!"

Chuck replied, "Now just one minute, who do you think you are…"

Al cut him off again and replied, "Someone who's getting really tired of this place," and walked out.

Bill looked at Chuck and said, "You're not having any luck at all lately are you?"

Chuck replied, "Al's right, I should've kissed his ass. Ron's the only guy to come along, ever that showed any ability to control the dogs. I should have driven him home to Illinois personally if that's what he needed. Bill, I have to get him back here, somehow!"

Bill replied, "Why don't you start by calling the police, have you gone to his hotel?"

Chuck responded, "No, but I did call the hotel, he hasn't checked out."

Bill replied, "You really need to change Chuck, if you cared about Ron you would've been to the hotel checking on him the first day he was gone, you're really not a people person are you?"

Chuck looked up and replied, "I'm afraid not Bill, I never have been."

Bill replied, "Why don't you go to the hotel, I'll call the police and if you see Ron, please apologize to the man."

Ron and Angela were walking toward the hotel restaurant, hand in hand. Ron stopped dead in his tracks when he spotted Katie standing at the entrance.

Katie yelled out, "Daddy!" and ran towards him. Ron started running towards her and stooped down as he got close. Katie jumped into his arms so hard it knocked him over and the two of them lay on the floor hugging one another. Everyone around started applauding and Ron looked up at Angie with tears in his eyes and said, "Thank you baby."

Angela broke into tears and Katie asked, "What's wrong Mommy, how come you're crying?"

Angela replied, "Nothing sweetie."

Ron added, "Nothing now! C'mon group hugs, I really missed you guy's!"

They found a table and ordered breakfast, Katie sat on her Dad's lap the entire time and fed him every bite. He hadn't eaten properly for a few days now and although this did slow him down he didn't care, Ron was thrilled to be with his family again.

Jane was going on and on about all the things she wanted to do while in New York. Being a thirty something divorcee, she had intended to get into some trouble while she was here. The Hard Rock café was first on her list along with a cute bartender she had noticed at the hotel bar when they checked in last night.

Ron did his best to get them caught up with all that happened on the job. He added, "I really miss those lunches with you guys at Chucky Cheese."

Angela rolled her eyes and Ron realized it was a mistake as Katie went through the rest of breakfast demanding dinner at Chucky's.

Angela finally turned the subject to what they were going to do next.

Ron replied, "Well, no matter what, we're all here, together now and it's going to stay that way!" He added, "I think I should at least make an appearance at the office and let them know I'm alive. Tell them you guy's are here and put Chuck in his place, either I get a leave of absence or I quit.

Katie heard Chuck and started chanting, "Chucky, Chucky, Chucky!"

Angela could tell the subject was upsetting Ron, the last thing he wanted to do was quit. To change the subject she gently started running her foot up and down his leg from under the table, which immediately got his attention. Ron started to growl and Jane added, "Down tiger, get a room already."

Katie picked up her hand and made a clawing gesture then started to growl as well and added, "You tiger Daddy," and growled again

They started laughing out loud, Katie looked puzzled not really knowing what she had said but joined in the laughter.

Jane replied, "From the mouths of babes."

After settling down they agreed Ron would go to the office and the girls would take a walk around the neighborhood for a while.

Ron got up, paid the bill and headed for the circular door that led to the street. While halfway through the doorway he stopped for a moment, forgetting it was a circular door. He felt a thud as the man on the other side of the door hit his head on the glass. Ron didn't realize it but the man on the other side was Chuck, Ron quickly exited the door and rushed down the street.

As Chuck entered the lobby he rubbed his head and commented, "Damn tourists, can't even use a door."

He made his way to the front desk, got on line and waited to speak to the desk clerk. At the same time, Angela and the girls ended up on line just behind him. They waited for a few minutes and Katie started going on again about

Chucky Cheese. She chanted, "Chucky, Chucky, Chucky!" and got louder with each Chucky.

Chuck turned around, didn't say anything but was obviously irritated.

Jane quickly commented, "She's just a little girl for crying out loud, she's excited!"

Chuck continued ignoring them and Angela added, "Let's not bother the man," and raised her foot pretending to kick him in his butt. They laughed, Katie tried to copy her Mom and just missed kicking Chuck's leg. They laughed again as Chuck made it to the front of the line and asked the clerk, "I wonder if you can help me, I'm looking for an employee of mine who is staying here. He hasn't been to the office for a few days now and I'm concerned for his safety."

Jane overheard him and quietly told Angela to listen.

He continued, "His name is Ron Miller."

The girls looked at each other, wide eyed with amazement.

Angela spoke first, "How do you know my husband!"

Chuck turned around and asked, "Your husband, Ron Miller is your husband?"

Angela recognized his voice and started in right away. She added, "Your that cold hearted, insensitive, self serving boss of his, Chuck, right."

Chuck started to reply but Angela cut in and continued, "Do you know what you've put us through. How can you be so heartless."

Chuck cut in this time, noticing that they had the undivided attention of everyone in the lobby.

He replied, "Can we continue this conversation a little more privately, we really need to talk."

Angela agreed, Jane kept Katie occupied while Chuck and Angela continued.

Chuck added, "First, please tell me Ron is alright, I have to admit I did not handle your husband's problem very well, I deeply regret any inconvenience this has caused you all."

Angela replied, "Well you should apologize, my husband has worked his butt off for you. In spite of you he's whipping your little team of baboons into shape and how do you repay him, by putting us through hell, you have some nerve."

Angela caught herself and realized she was going to lose control if she continued.

Chuck saw the opportunity to get a word in so he replied, "I want you to do whatever you need to do."

He stopped when he noticed Angela was becoming tense and her hand was balling up into a fist so he added, "Perhaps I should rephrase that, I want you and Ron to take whatever time you need to get your affairs in order. If you need to return home so be it, if there's anything I can do to help please let me know. Perhaps you can take some time and start looking for your new home here in New York."

Angela replied," I'm glad to hear you've come to your senses."

Angela could hear the urgency in Chuck's voice and knew he sincerely wanted or perhaps needed Ron to stay. She decided to raise the stakes a little and increase her husband's value.

She replied, "Well, he's on his way up to the office right now, if you can convince him to stay then I'm game. Good luck with that though, he's really pissed off at you."

Chuck tried to maintain a calm demeanor but was never very good at hiding his emotions. Angela could read his face like an open book and knew she had him in panic mode. He quickly said his goodbyes and rushed back to the office, Angela couldn't help but laugh as Chuck started to run, he was slow and kind of waddled like a duck.

Jane came up behind Angela and commented, "Is it me or is that man running with a full load in his diaper."

Ron arrived at the office, Gertie the receptionist was the first to greet him and said, "Ron, where have you been, the entire office has been worried sick about you, are you alright?"

Before Ron could reply, Bill entered the lobby and added, "Am I ever glad to see you, we really need to talk!"

Ron replied, "You guy's are going to make me blush, I missed you too."

He gave Gertie a hug and was rushed into Bill's office.

Bill asked Ron, "So, are you alright, you scared the hell out of all of us when you disappeared."

Ron replied, "My girls surprised me and showed up at the hotel. Besides, I've been doing a lot of soul searching lately, I'm not sure I can continue working for Chuck. Between you and me he's the biggest butt hole I've ever worked for."

Bill laughed then responded, "I can't argue with that!"

Ron continued, "He's going to have to let me do what I need to do in Illinois or I'm here to quit."

Bill replied, "Between you and me the old man has been crapping his pants since you stopped coming in. Ron, you're in the driver's seat right now, no one has ever handled the dog pound the way you have and Chuck can't afford to lose you, none of us can."

Just then, Al and Renee barged into Bill's office, Renee couldn't hide her emotions and started tearing up.

She told Ron, "I was sure you left us Ron, please say your staying."

Al added, "It's only been a few days but the knuckleheads are trying to take over again, please say your not leaving us."

Ron started to tell them, "I'd like to stay but my family needs me too, I need to talk to Chuck, where the hell is he?"

Then Chuck arrived and replied, "I'm here Ron," he put out his hand and added, "I am sorry for being a stubborn, self serving old fool. I realize I should never have asked you to put your job above the needs of your family. I was wrong, can you forgive me?"

Ron shook his hand and replied, "Does this mean I can take care of business at home and come back when I can?"

Chuck replied, "Of course Ron, of course. Please understand though, the dogs are starting to act up again, they're reverting back to their old ways without you around."

Renee added, "Frank stopped returning my calls again."

Al cut in, "And Greg is still Greg but at least he's consistent."

Chuck continued, "Take whatever time you need but remember us, we need you. Now please tell me you'll stay."

Ron replied, "Of course I'll stay, but there is one condition."

Chuck looked at Ron and replied, "What's this going to cost me?"

Ron pulled Chuck aside and whispered in his ear, at first Chuck scowled and looked alarmed but thought about it and said, "If you can pull that off, you deserve it, we have a deal! It'll never happen though!"

Ron replied, "We'll see!"

The room erupted with excitement and could be heard all the way back in the dispatch area. Ron advised Renee to get the word out, there will be hell to pay for anyone who started slacking off.

Renee replied, "I know exactly who needs to hear that!"

After spending a couple of hours in the office and refusing to tell anyone what it was he agreed to, Ron rejoined his family back at the hotel.

After lunch they spent the afternoon taking in the sites of New York. They went to Times Square, Ron showed Katie the biggest Toys R Us anywhere and went for a ride on their huge indoor Ferris wheel. They followed it up with a trip to the famous FAO Schwarz toy store. They almost thought it was a mistake when Katie started asking for one of the five hundred dollar Barbie dolls but Jane distracted her while they bought her one of the more affordable ones.

Later that night, Ron and Angela got their alone time, all night and Angela finally made him pay for leaving her in Illinois for so long. Ron didn't mind at all and reasoned he needed the workout.

The following day, Ron, Angela and Katie rented a car and decided to get out of the city for awhile. Angela was already getting tired of the crowds, she described it was like everywhere you wanted to put your foot down, three other people were competing for the same spot at the same time. While at breakfast, their waitress mentioned a great zoo in the Bronx. Katie overheard and loved the idea, they figured it would be a nice change of pace so they were on their way.

Once on the highway, they were immediately stuck in traffic, bumper to bumper and then missed their exit when a very large truck blocked their exit. After hours of frustration however they turned off of the highway and found themselves in a wooded area. They followed a couple of traffic circles and came to an opening that let out onto a bridge, then a sign that read, "Welcome to City Island."

Angela looked around and fell in love with what she saw. It was a seaport with lots of boats in the water and seagulls in the air. They proceeded down City Island avenue and saw lots of shops and restaurants with a lot fewer people around.

Ron was so frustrated with the drive he pulled into the first parking spot he could find and raced out of the car, almost ready to kneel down and kiss the ground.

Katie immediately started asking, "Where are the aminals, I want to see the aminals, where are they?"

Ron and Angela looked at each other, Angela spoke first and said, "That had to be the worst drive of my life."

Ron replied, "I've never seen traffic like that, ever!"

Katie continued, "I want aminals, where are the aminals?"

A passerby overheard Katie's ranting about the animals and commented, "You must be here for the fair." He added, "It's a ways down the street, you may want to drive."

Ron replied, "After the drive we just had, no way, we'll walk, I don't care how far it is."

The man replied, "Suit yourself."

Angela added, "Please tell me they have animals."

They started walking and Angela started developing a fondness for the island. Along the way they branched off of the main street and realized City Island really was an island. There were quaint little shops, bungalows with their own docks and boats in their slips. They noticed it was considerably quieter than the city and smelled a lot better too.

They arrived at the fair, which for Katie was close enough to a zoo. She rode the pony and must have fed every animal in the petting zoo.

Along the way back, they started discussing Ron's relapse into drinking. Ron admitted he was scared at how quickly it hit him and how powerless he was to stop it. He admitted he had to find a meeting he liked.

Angela replied, "You only tried one meeting though Ron," with a smile that made it difficult to argue with.

Ron noticed that one of Katie's shoes were untied so he stopped, knelt down to tie her shoe. As he knelt down, Angela exclaimed, "Oh my, Ron, look," and pointed at a sign down the street.

Ron immediately recognized it as an Alcoholics Anonymous sign, in front of an old church. Without a word, Angela started walking towards the church leaving Ron with no way out.

Ron replied, "Come on Angie, it's getting late, Katie will be falling asleep soon."

Angie didn't stop until she reached the front of the church and was greeted by a few men and women who were standing out front. Ron joined her and one of the men asked, "Can we help you?"

Ron recognized they were holding coffee cups so felt comfortable asking, "Is this an AA meeting."

One of the men replied, "Sure is, does someone have a desire to stop drinking today?"

Ron admitted, "I've been sober for three years now but relapsed recently."

The man replied, "My name is John and I'm an alcoholic, welcome Ron."

The other men joined in and welcomed him then John announced, "We have a meeting getting ready to start but I'm afraid the misses won't be able to sit in. He whispered in Ron's ear that there was an ice cream shop around the corner, perhaps that would entertain the little one for a while.

Angela overheard and replied, "That will be perfect Ron, please go inside, we'll be fine."

Ron explained to John all that he had been going through, the pressures of the new job, the problems with the stalled move from Illinois. John listened intently as Ron described the one meeting he attended in the city. Throughout the entire meeting he heard only one person talk about drinking, it was not what he was used to and it left him frustrated.

John explained to Ron that there are a lot of meetings in New York. He could expect to find some meetings like that but if he looked he'd find a lot of old school AA meetings as well.

He added, "In spite of that one meeting, there must have been something you could identify with. Even if you can't think of anything, look at it like this. Say you're on a sinking ship, you just landed in the water and a purple life preserver passes by. You hate the color purple but it may be

132

the only life preserver left, it's the difference between you drowning or surviving Ron, what would you do?"

Ron looked at John and admitted, "I guess it can be that simple."

John gave Ron a meeting book with listings for all the meetings in the area, he circled some old school type meetings he knew of in New York. John also gave Ron his phone number and had at least six other members give their numbers as well then told him, "If you feel the need to drink, call one of us, don't worry about how late it is, just call us before you drink!"

By the end of the meeting Ron was feeling pretty good and headed back to Angie and Katie. Katie was still enjoying her ice cream cone so Ron ordered a cone, smashed it into hers and said "Smoosh!"

Katie laughed and said, "Daddy, you silly!"

Angie asked about the meeting and Ron replied, "It was a lot better than the one in the city, all the speakers talked about was drinking and John was a great guy to talk to. I really feel good."

Angie replied, "I'm so glad you feel that way, can I show you something?"

They left the ice cream parlor and Ron put Katie on his shoulders as they walked towards the water. Angela explained that they walked around for a while before going for ice cream. They reached the end of the block and Angela pointed to a cute little house on the bay with a for sale sign on it. The sun was just starting to set and it looked like something out of a Norman Rockwell painting.

She added, "Look, a white picket fence and all, what do you think Ron."

Ron replied, "I love it honey, let's do it."

Chapter 5 - The Ring

It took a couple of weeks but Ron was able to pull everything together. After returning to Illinois, he and Angela had found a new real estate agency. Their new agent decided to lease their house and handle any problems until it could be sold.

They moved into their cute little house by the bay on City Island, Katie was thrilled when she woke up her first morning there and realized she could feed the ducks in her own back yard.

Ron was happy when he learned he could catch an express bus to the city right from the island, it was a deciding factor for him. The memory of that first awful drive to the island was still very fresh in his mind and he had no desire to recreate it every morning and night.

So after an hour on the bus, Ron found himself in his office once again. Everyone was thrilled he had finally returned, especially Bill who had to share Ron's responsibilities along with Al while he was away. Bill came into his office and started bringing him up to speed.

He explained to Ron that they had hired him an additional tech but not to be too excited. Bill added, "This kid is Sam, the delivery guy's son. His interview was horrible, he couldn't trace wiring at all and was clumsy as hell with tools. Somehow Sam pulled some strings and got him hired."

Ron replied, "So long as were talking about pulling strings, how the hell did I end up with him? Didn't you have an open requisition too?"

They both smiled and Bill added, "You had to be here buddy, you like a challenge don't you?"

Ron replied, "I have about as many challenged individuals as I can handle right now and that doesn't even include our wonderful customers or our fearless leader."

Bill responded, "Witless warrior is more like it."

They laughed and Bill continued updating him with various customer issues. The machine at Investco has to be relocated asap. A Force of one still calls the office almost everyday but that's nothing new, the owner is a butt hole however he's good for comic relief.

Ron added, "That's the guy who sounds like a woman, right?"

Bill added, "You can't make this stuff up, we should write a book. Who would believe a neurotic, effeminate assertiveness trainer?"

Al walked in just as Bill was wrapping things up and told Ron, "Am I ever glad to see you again!"

Bill added, "I can vouch for that, Al's been taking a beating while you were gone. As usual, Chuck has been running like hell from anything that resembles a problem."

Al cut in, "I've been the acting manager and specialist while you were away."

Ron asked, "Has Chuck compensated you at all for the extra work?"

Al replied, "Chuck said he would talk to corporate about a special stipend they used to offer for situations like this."

Ron and Bill looked at one another then burst into laughter.

Al asked, "Did I miss something?"

Ron replied, "I'm sorry Al, that's the same line he used on me, remember? The real estate fiasco with Angie and I."

Al rolled his eyes and added, "Son of a …!"

Bill added, "Don't worry Al, I'm sure Chuck will give you at least two, That a boy's, maybe even a, Way to go!"

Al replied, "So long as were on the subject of Chuck, I have to ask you Ron, just before you left for

Illinois you pulled him aside and whispered something in his ear. Something he wasn't too happy about, something about a price for whipping the dog pound into shape, what's up with that?"

Bill added, "That's a great question Al, I've been dying to find that out myself, so what's up with that Ron?"

Ron replied, "Now guy's, I'm kind of sworn to secrecy about that, I promise you'll find out soon enough. Let's just say Chuck may have to pay a heavy price for keeping me here."

After a few minutes, Bill excused himself as Al and Ron sat and went over plans for the day. Al brought Ron up to speed and admitted going over the spreadsheet and numbers that were on his desk while he was away. They were a few weeks old now but Al saw a huge cost discrepancy in Greg's parts.

Al explained, "We know that Greg almost never orders or replaces parts. If you add up those numbers he has a ton of parts he's never returned. How does a guy who never orders parts have a problem with returned parts? It doesn't add up!"

Ron replied, "That's a good catch Al, it could be an error but you might be onto something. I'll look into it but thanks."

In the mean time Bill was telling me about a relocation we need to do at Investco. Their twelfth floor machine is now in the middle of a demolished room, Oscar's crying to sales that it's been down for a month, is it me or is Oscar a total idiot? If he told us about this before he demolished the room we could have moved it before hand."

Al smiled and replied, "You called it right, Oscar's a total idiot."

Ron added, "Can you handle that for me, sales is crying it needs to be done today, maybe you can take the new guy with you, Sam's kid."

Al replied, "Don't get me started, that kid is like a ticking time bomb waiting to go off. He's on his way to training as we speak but he's going to be a serious problem for all of us. He acts like he knows everything already but he knows nothing."

Ron added, "I heard his interview was terrible too, nice to know nothing's changed while I was gone, their still hiring boobs."

Al replied, "And sending them to us!"

After a few minutes Al started heading to Investco and Ron began getting back to work, he had a full day ahead of him just responding to Emails but put a big red circle around the numbers that Al pointed out.

Al arrived at Investco and had Oscar show him the machine. Oscar was whining as usual, this time about the machine being down for almost a month. Al reminded him that they received the request to move the machine late last week.

Oscar replied, "I don't know who slipped up but I need this machine back in operation right away! Let me show you where it has to go!"

Oscar walked Al through the remains of the room, it was a mess. There was broken sheetrock and plaster dust everywhere with pieces of pipe all over the floor. Oscar led Al to a doorway that led to a narrow hall. Al immediately realized that the hallway was too narrow, the machine would fit but it would be a nightmare to service.

Instead of arguing with Oscar, Al got on the phone with Ron, who got on the phone with Chuck, who got on the phone with Sales, who got on the phone with Oscar.

They tried their best to stop the move but in the end, as usual the customer won and Al started dismantling the machine.

In the mean time, Mike, Brad and John were finishing up a tough day of their own. One of the machines

Mike acquired from Tom was falling apart, it needed to be field stripped and rebuilt. So after a long day of rebuilding the machine they decided to head to the gym and probably Rosie's afterward.

John had just finished some heavy lifts and got up to stretch when someone walking by said, "Excuse me." John moved out of the guy's way and bumped into another man, a huge guy, causing him to drop a small weight he was carrying onto his foot.

With a heavy Russian accent the guy went off on John. John said he was sorry, it was an accident and tried to show him the other guy who started the whole thing, but he was gone.

The big Russian started pushing John and John quickly lost his temper. Now it was a full-fledged argument and both had to be restrained. Brad and Mike forgot how strong John was and had problems holding him back. The big Russian had three guy's holding him and they were having problems as well.

The big Russian yelled at John, "I think I have to kick your ass tough guy, what do you think of that."

John replied, "OK Boris, anytime you think you're big enough!"

The big Russian shouted, "I meet you here tomorrow, six pm, I kick your ass in the ring."

The gym had a boxing ring in the back and they ran amateur boxing matches every Friday night.

John shot back, "I'll be here, just don't wimp out you douche!"

The big Russian looked puzzled and asked one of his restrainers, "What is douche?" When he was told what it was he started fuming again. He pointed at John and said, "I am going to cripple you wise guy, be here or I will find you."

The big Russian picked up a weight and threw it at John like it was an empty soda can, just missing him and then stormed out of the gym.

Mike and Brad were still holding John back and let him go when they realized the Russian was gone, that and someone in the gym yelled out, "Get a room."

Brad told John, "What are you going to do? Did you see the size of that guy?" Mike added, "And he was pissed."

John replied, "Come on you guy's, have a little faith here, I can kick his butt."

Mike and Brad shook their head's in disbelief and left it at that for now.

They eventually left the gym and stopped at Rosie's to cool off. They ran into Al, who had finished up at Investco and was sitting at the bar filling out a raffle ticket.

Brad explained to Mike, "Every week the electronics place around the corner runs a raffle, you put the ticket in a jar and every Friday they pull out a winner."

Al changed the subject and told them, "I had to do a relocation at Investco, Oscar stuck it to us again. That machine on the twelfth floor we haven't had calls on in a month, turns out the copy room is being dismantled, you should see it, the room looks like a bomb went off. Anyway, the copier is in the hallway now. I told Ron the hallway was too narrow but he couldn't stop it. Oscar cried to sales, sales cried to the big guys and we're stuck with it. It may not be too bad though, Oscar insists the hallway is never used. We'll see, I've learned to never trust that guy."

Al asked what they were up to and Mike replied, "Getting into trouble as usual."

Al responded, "That doesn't sound good."

John started getting fired up again and ordered a shot of Jack Daniels.

Brad told him, "Hold on there Rocky, that's not going to help."

Mike added, "Speaking of Rocky, funny you came up with the name Boris for that guy," then gave his best Bullwinkle impression.

They laughed and Al asked, "What happened?"

Brad started explaining about the gym and the big Russian, Mike motioned how huge the guy was.

Brad asked, "John, what are you going to do, you can't take that guy, both of us together couldn't take him."

Mike added, "My nephew is a pharmacist, maybe he can get me some chloroform or something."

John replied, "Thanks, but I'm sure they check for that stuff, don't worry, I'll kick his butt."

Brad and Mike looked at each other and shook their heads again, Brad motioned his hand across his throat as if to cut it.

The next day, news started spreading through the company about John's upcoming fight.

Ron pleaded with John to simply not show up. Joyce, the sales reps made it a point to meet up with John for lunch and was very upset. She relayed a message from her team leader Ivanna and said if the ruskie harmed Johns cute little tush she'd kick the guy's butt herself.

Renee was trying to leave John and Brad alone so she asked Mike to take a call at Investco. Although Mike wanted to stay with Brad and John, he gladly pitched in to help.

The call was on the same machine that Al had done the relocation on the day before. They had a problem with dirty copies.

When Mike arrived onsite he saw that Al wasn't exaggerating, the room the copier was in before was nothing more than sheet metal girders, debris and partially erected sheetrock walls.

The machine was now in a narrow hallway pressed up against a wall. Mike squeezed himself between the machine and the wall until he finally got enough space to pull the rear covers off. The machine was full of dust and required some cleaning. Unfortunately the space was so tight, every time he had to work in the front he had to push the machine back. Every time he had to work in the back he had to move the machine to the front. Al was right, Oscar screwed them again.

He hooked up the vacuum cleaner and moved the machine to the back again. With the front covers open there was hardly any room to work. The space between the front covers and the wall when the covers were open was very narrow, if someone had to get by they would have to be pretty skinny.

Mike got started cleaning and was hoping to finish early to spend time with John. "The poor guy," he thought to himself, "I wouldn't want to be in his shoes."

The cleaning was going well and Mike thought to himself, "This may not be too bad, it's a pain in the butt getting the machine set up for service, but once that's done it's manageable."

Just then, he heard an elevator door open at the end of the hallway and a lunch cart made it's way out of the elevator. Then he heard on the loudspeaker that the lunch cart was in the hallway and open for business.

He looked and wondered where this guy's customers could possibly come from, then realized the only door was the one he came in from, at the opposite end of the hallway and that put him immediately between them.

With that, the door swung open and a huge crowd of people tried squeezing through it at once. It was like a herd of cattle, a stampede heading right for him. Before Mike could get out of the way a huge bulk of a woman hit one of the front covers, pinning him between the herd and the machine. Mike thought he heard the woman yell in a deep, slow motion voice, "Hold on to my prune danish Habib," as she whizzed by him.

He managed to turn his head a few times and realized everyone in the herd was at least two hundred pounds.

The crowd finally passed him and Mike found himself lying on the floor. As he slowly pulled himself up he realized the machine was pressed against the wall again, he saw the crowd swarming the lunch cart and he felt sorry for Habib, the vendor.

As the crowd started making it's way back, Mike got out of the way but they resembled a calm, grazing herd this time. The woman with the danish commented, "You should move this machine, it's in a bad spot." Mike could barely make out what she was saying and thought he saw a piece of danish sticking out of her mouth.

Mike replied, "And you should drop a few hundred pounds you beast."

She heard him and tried to turn around but was unable to, the crowd just carried her along. Mike calmed himself and finished cleaning the machine.

He found the bathroom, started washing up and realized he had to go, so he found an open stall. While he was in the stall his phone rang, it was Al.

He answered the phone and said, "Hello," just as someone else was coming into the bathroom.

The guy who had just come into the bathroom responded, "Hello."

Mike told him, "I'm not talking to you," and heard Al on the other end say, "Why not, what did I do."

Mike tried answering the phone again and said, "Hello," but the guy who had just entered the bathroom said in a frustrated voice, "Look, I don't know who you are back there but I'm not in the habit of meeting people in the men's bathroom you pervert," then Mike heard him leave and the door close behind him.

By now Al had hung up so Mike finished, got out to the hallway and called Al back.

Al sounded a little upset and asked Mike what was wrong, why the attitude. He had a good laugh once Mike explained and said, "You just can't make this stuff up."

Al told Mike they were heading to Rosie's and to meet them there when he could.

Mike made it to Rosie's just in time, they had to leave for the gym soon. John was upstairs limbering up and Al was at the bar with Brad when he arrived.

Mike asked them, "How's our boy?"

Brad responded, "He can't wait to get there, he really thinks he has a shot.

I saw him like this when we were in the Marine's and assigned to Desert storm. A couple of times when we were under attack, John was plain fearless, he has the heart of a warrior when he needs it, but sometimes he's just not realistic."

Just then, John made his way down the staircase, the guys started mouthing the theme song to Rocky, "da da, da da da , da da da da da da."

John was really pumped and making swinging motions with his hands, you couldn't help but admire the guy, full of heart, or something else.

They made their way to the gym and heard lots of cheers for John once they got through the main entrance. Apparently word spread like wildfire, there were techs and dispatchers from other groups, sales reps and some customers as well, all gathered in support of John.

Brad and John went to the dressing room while Mike stayed near the ring and started unpacking the towels and water bottles. Al disappeared into the crowd to talk to Ron just as Gil from Sloppy Copy joined Mike at ringside. Mike welcomed him and said, "I guess you heard the news, John is fighting tonight."

Gil replied, "Yeah I heard, I come here every week. Did you know the Russian mob is into this place, they run bets on the side. I saw on the fight card that John was fighting Vlad the impaler, are you guy's crazy? They usually have to carry guys out on a stretcher after Vlad is through with them, and those are the guys he likes."

Mike suddenly recalled what the big Russian said in the gym, "I am going to cripple you."

Mike said to Gil, "Oh no, Gil, how do we stop this?

John thinks he's walking into an amateur match, this guy wants to hurt him bad!"

Gil replied, "Vlad always plays around with his opponents the first couple of rounds, I think they drive up the bets like that. It's the third round when he busts them up."

Just then the lights started dimming and an announcer started entering the ring, he was sort of comical looking, a short, pudgy Hispanic guy.

Gil said, "Good luck," and made his way into the crowd.

Mike saw Brad and John making their way to the ring as the announcer started introducing John to the crowd. He held his hand over the microphone and Mike overheard him ask the timekeeper, "What do you know about this guy?"

The time keeper replied, "I heard Vlad say he would smack him around like he was his bitch."

The announcer continued, "Ladies and Gentlemen, put your hands together and welcome Puta Grande."

Again Mike overheard the timekeeper tell the announcer, "I'll call the ambulance now, Vlad really hates this guy."

As everyone was cheering, Brad and John finally arrived at ringside.
It was obvious John was pumped up but had no idea what was really going on.

Mike told Brad, "I just saw Gil, we have to stop this."

John replied first, "What, are you kidding, listen to this crowd, I'm going to beat the crap out of this guy."

Mike whispered to Brad what Gil had told him earlier.

Brad went blank, then responded, "The Russian mob?"

John looked at Brad and said, "What did you say?"

Then Mike explained the rest. He told them, "This Russian is a regular here, they rig bets by getting guys like us to fight him. Gil said if he likes you they carry you out on a stretcher, if not," and left it at that. Gil also said it was usually the third round when Vlad went to work."

Just then the Russian was announced and entered the ring, he was staring hard at John and motioned his hand across his throat, then pointed right at him. The crowd went crazy and started cheering him on.

Then the ring Girl came into the ring carrying a big sign with the number one, she was gorgeous and wearing a tiny two piece thong. She winked at John as she walked by him and John told Brad, "She's hot for me, did you see that?"

Brad wondered if she would still like him in a wheelchair.

The ring girl made her exit while the announcer called Vlad and John to the center of the ring. Suddenly John wasn't feeling so cocky and as they got to the center he tried calming Vlad down.

He said, "You know I was kidding in the gym right, just a little fun."

The Russian just stared at him and said nothing. At the break, they touched gloves and Vlad pushed John back so hard he almost landed back in his corner. Then the Russian pointed at John, stared at him and said, "Douche!"

Suddenly the bell rang, Vlad came out charging and took a swing at John with his right, John backed up and caught Vlad with a right of his own.

It didn't faze the Russian at all but John felt good, at least he connected.

The entire first round went the same way, the Russian never really connected but John never hurt him either. Finally the bell rang and John came back to his corner.

John said, "This guy is slow, I can take him."

Mike reminded him what Gil had said about the third round.

The ring girl made her way around the ring, winking at John again.

John said, "I'm going to win this and hook up with her too, she's hot."

With that, the bell rang and round two was underway. This time the big Russian started with a couple of jabs that connected. John tried to respond but couldn't hit him, suddenly it was starting to feel like a different fight.

John did his best to keep away from Vlad and was almost cornered twice. But after keeping away for awhile, the Russian finally cornered him, then nailed him with a heavy right hand that spun John around. As John was spinning around he managed to raise his hand and caught Vlad in the face with a right of his own, almost by accident.

The shot probably hurt John's hand more than it hurt Vlad and Mike saw John wince in pain. John was starting to feel light headed just as Vlad caught him with a left and then, finally, the bell rang. John never felt more relieved.

John staggered back to his corner and had to be helped to his stool, he was groggy and not thinking clearly.

He kept saying, "Did you see that shot I gave him? Pow, right in the face man, he felt that."

Mike and Brad looked at one another, they knew the shot John was talking about was an accidental shot. John just happened to have his hand up as he was spinning around, it hurt John more than Vlad.

They thought, "How can we stop this?"

Then Al came up behind them and said, "Do you guys have a death wish? Get John out of there."

John turned around and saw Al, he was in a daze and said, "Al, baby, my man, watch this, I'm gonna get this guy," and got up off of his stool.

Al grabbed his gloves and told him, "John, this has to end right now, the guy is playing with you. You're his bitch and he's going to take you out, this round, get it!"

John tried to pull away, but Al would not let go.

Then the ring girl came around, she winked again and as she passed behind John, Al let him go. John was pulling away so hard and was so dazed, he spun around and ran into her. The ring girl's knees buckled and the sign came down right on top of John's head.

He briefly looked into the ring girl's eyes, gave the goofiest smile and went unconscious, with that the ring girl landed right on top of him.

Brad, Mike and Al ran into the ring and helped the ring girl up, almost seeming to forget about John. The ring girl was all right, she smiled and added, "Aren't you forgetting about your friend?" While she was walking away she shook her head and could be heard saying, "Men."

By now, John was conscious but wobbly and as they started helping John up off of the floor, Vlad was heard telling the referee to continue the fight.

The referee told him twice, "Forget about it, John could not fight in this condition."

Vlad must have blown a fuse and started going off. He started charging towards Mike who was the closest to him, when out of nowhere came Kelly, the new girl. She slid under the ropes, quickly got to her feet and placed herself between Mike and Vlad.

Vlad didn't care who was in front of him and took a monstrous swing at Kelly.

Kelly ducked, came back up and caught Vlad with a left then a right uppercut.

Vlad's head snapped back and down he went, totally unconscious.

The crowd cheered wildly and Mike gave Kelly the biggest hug, which he quickly realized was a mistake when she hugged him back.

Mike thought to himself, "She's as strong as she looks."

Al and Brad quickly joined them in the middle of the ring and the referee announced the match a draw with Kelly declared the unofficial winner.

Mike told Kelly she had to join them at Rosie's later and Kelly replied, "I'll be there but I have to take care of something first."

The boys arrived at Rosie's just as a full blown party was starting. A lot of Rosie's customers were joining in the celebration but the AYS presence was overwhelming.

John was trying to impress everyone he could with his side of the story but they all replied the same, "You got knocked out by the ring girl tough guy."

Al and Gil came up to John, Brad and Mike and told John he should plant a big wet one on Gil.

John made a face like he had just sucked on a lemon and replied, "Ewwwww,"

Al explained, "A few of the ring girl's work at the strip club that Gil hangs out at. Gil knew you would probably die tonight so he got one of them to switch with the girl who was supposed to be covering your fight. We arranged the whole thing, all I had to do was get you to bang in to her, she took care of the rest."

John was speechless but Mike and Brad started high fiving Gil and Al.

After awhile John went back to reminding them that he wanted to hook up with the ring girl, "We had a connection, she kept winking at me," he kept repeating.

Gil responded, "Wake up, you still don't get it do you?"

Then the crowd started getting noisy. Joyce, Stu and a bunch of others started mouthing the Rocky theme music.

It was the ring girl and Kelly, they were holding hands as they made their way to the bar. Gil gave the ring girl, whose name they now found out was Rhonda, a huge hug and told her, "You were fantastic in there." Brad and Mike agreed and gave her huge hugs as well.

Mike looked at Kelly and said, "I owe you big, that guy would have killed me in there. Where did you learn to fight like that?"

Kelly replied, "I've been amateur boxing for about two years now, I'll be entering the golden gloves soon, I hope."

They all gathered around Kelly and Rhonda, gave them hugs and thanked them.

John looked up at Rhonda and put his hand on his head where the sign hit him and said, "Thanks, I think."

Rhonda replied, "Anytime John," and pinched his cheek. She added, "I hope you know he was going to put you in the hospital, Vlad is really crazy."

John told Rhonda he was hoping to catch up with her after the fight.

Kelly cut in and replied, "Hey, get your own."

Rhonda added, "I like it a little rough there John, I'm not sure you could handle me." At that Kelly and Rhonda gave each other a hug and the boy's ordered a round of drinks for the real heroes of the night, the girls.

Mike remembered Al was entering a raffle the day before and asked how he did.

Al pulled an IPod out of his pocket and said he won.

Mike replied, "That was good luck."

Then Brad cut in, " It helps if you have a system."

John quickly explained," It helps if you fix copiers all day and stuff the raffle box with a hundred copies of your ticket, you can't lose." They all laughed, Mike and Kelly started debating which one of them would stuff the raffle box next.

Ron and Bill had a great view of the crowd from upstairs. Ron was beaming with pride at his group of techs.

Bill commented, "Looks like you have a team starting to form down there, how the hell did that happen?" and admitted his crew wanted little to do with each other.

Ron admitted he wasn't sure if he knew but would enjoy it while he could.

Mike was joking with Joyce who joined them at the bar and suddenly saw a familiar face in the crowd. It was the huge woman from Investco, the one with the prune danish who knocked him down in the hallway. You could tell she was angry and heading right for him. She was going on about calling her a beast and that Oscar told her she might find him there.

Mike got up and started walking fast around the bar, gently pushing his way through the crowd. He kept egging her on and was having fun with her but hoped she never got her fat stubby hands on him.

Mike told her, "Danish here, get your fresh danish," and kept running.

She kept after him saying, "I'm going to get you, you son of a b…."

Mike continued, mooing along the way.

Everyone was laughing and enjoying the show. Mike had already told the guys how she ran him over for a freaking danish so they sympathized.

Ron looked at Bill, pointed at Mike and told him, "I think I may need to work on that ones peoples skills."

Just then the jukebox started playing, "Who let the dogs out," and everyone started singing along, by now the prune danish lady had given up and Mike bought her a drink.

Kelly looked at Mike and said, "I think I'm going to like it here."

Mike replied, "I know I do."

He gave her a hug and they just sang and howled to the music, along with everyone else.

Chapter 6 - The Tough Sell

Mike stepped off of the lunar rover, he had been dispatched to Camp Aldrin and had to repair an ore extractor that had jammed. The extractor was the size of an earth sized dump truck and he knew it had to be something large that stopped it. He arrived onsite and quickly realized a relay had shorted out. He ordered the part and Sam, the lunar delivery driver quickly delivered the part but threw it out of his delivery chute.

In the weightlessness of the lunar environment the part started sailing off into space. Mike keyed his microphone to contact his dispatcher Renee when out of nowhere he saw someone in a spacesuit with a Jamaican flag emblem and dreadlocks protruding from his helmet jump up in time to retrieve it. He brought the part over to Mike and heard the man say, "Wh'appen Mike, dat man be crazy. Why he be cut'n ya like dat. Don't stress boy, I got your back."

It was Roger, up here?

As Roger bounced lazily off into the lunar horizon, Mike saw puffs of smoke drifting up from his helmet.

Mike installed the relay and got the rover working again. Before giving it the command to move forward he thought it would be a good idea to look at the front bucket, "Something large had to stop this thing," he thought and didn't want to smoke another relay. He got to the front and observed a large slab like rock. He immediately thought of the movie, "2001 A Space Odyssey," and wondered if something special like the monolith had been uncovered.

He commanded the extractor to reverse, which exposed the slab and realized it had some sort of writing or inscription on it. He pulled a brush out of his tool bag and gently started cleaning it. After exposing the letters, he stepped back and read the inscription.

He went down on one knee in shock and yelled out, "Ralph, you really did it, you bastard!" The slab read, "Here lies the final resting place of Alice Kramden." Mike then recalled Ed Norton and the Captain Video episodes then thought, "No, not Norton too, an accomplice?"

Just then he awoke and heard his alarm clock blaring. He fumbled around till he found it, shut it off then thought, "This late night TV has to stop, you think they can put the honeymooners on a little earlier!"

Mike had been working overtime on another of the machines he acquired from Greg and he was starting to not care for the account very much. Ron and Al had warned him of the place when it was first assigned to him but there was no way to prepare for it, they were among the rudest of all the customers he had met so far.

The name of the account was, "A Force of One," they did assertiveness training for people who felt like they were getting pushed around a lot.

The owner could not have been more than five feet tall with a small frame and a very effeminate way about him. In spite of his feminine demeanor Mike doubted if he was gay, in his office he had a picture of himself with his wife and three kids.

The operator Gary was a young guy, most definitely gay and obviously had no intentions of hiding it.

The day before, Mike took his first call there, the operator placed calls every twenty minutes until he arrived onsite. Once onsite the operator watched everything he did and asked questions the entire time. At one point Mike told them the machine needed a part, he ordered it and told them he would be back the following day.

After leaving he got a call from Ron, who told him, "Bruce, the owner called and demanded Mike return and get the machine running no matter what."

Mike explained the situation to Ron who quickly replied, "Believe me, I know how those butt holes are, just go back for awhile and make nice, after an hour tell them you tried your best but without the part there is no way it can be fixed. If they call back again I'll tell them too bad."

So Mike went back, made nice and pretended to work on the machine. He found that the operator was an idiot and easily fooled into believing almost anything Mike told him about the machine. He was just Bruce, the owner's puppet and had do what he was told.

So Mike got out of bed and made his way into the city.

Back at the office, Ron had just arrived and sat at his desk, his morning was a little more hectic than Mike's. Earlier, when he was just about dressed for work, Angela had frantically called him into the living room. Katie was feeding the ducks in the back yard as usual when suddenly the entire yard was overrun with geese. Katie came running into the living room with what Ron later called, "Goose poopies," all over her shoes. Angela had a slightly different name for it once she started to clean Katie and the carpet.

After that excitement was over she asked Ron to consider not going to Rosie's anymore, considering his alcoholism. Ron assured her however that he was making meetings regularly again and felt no desire to drink. Even his new sponsor explained he could probably get away with going to a bar once in a while if it were truly for business purposes and more importantly, if he did not feel an urge to drink.

Ron added, "Honey, this team is really starting to come together, it feels good. I promise I'll only go there when something important is going on and I'll stop the instant I feel even the slightest urge to drink."

Angela reluctantly went along with it but added, "I really can't feel good about this Ron, I hope you know what you're doing."

As he sat at his desk, Chuck barged in and brought with him Ron's new technician, the delivery driver's son, Collin. He was back from training early and was actually thrown out of class for being obnoxious and difficult to train. Just as Al had warned him, Collin thought he knew everything already.

Chuck handed Collin's training folder to Ron and introduced them to each other.

Ron thumbed through the folder and asked Collin how he made it through training so quickly.

Collin quickly replied, "I'm that good!"

Ron laughed and added, "We'll see Collin, I've heard that before. Experience has taught me that people who think they know it all are usually the ones with the most to learn. I see here your interpretation of good includes obnoxious and abusive. You constantly interrupted the class to correct the instructor's and you damaged two machines. If I read this transcript correctly, no one in the class wanted to work with you, is this what you call good?"

Collin looked at Ron for a moment and replied, "Your instructor's don't know anything, I found a number of ways to improve your machines but they wouldn't admit I was right. The other trainees are idiots, sheep, they just follow along with everything the instructors say, no independent thought."

Ron quickly cut him off and replied, "If you're going to work on this team you'll have to make an effort to get along. Furthermore, are you aware it can take up to a year to learn how these machines work, even longer to figure out how they break."

Collin replied, "Maybe for you!"

Ron looked at Chuck and added, "What am I supposed to do with this guy?"

Chuck looked at Ron with a blank stare that said, "I've got nothing," then quickly excused himself.

Collin took a seat in front of Ron and started saying, "I can start taking calls right away but I'll require a territory close to the office. Also I'll need…"

Ron cut him off again, got right in his face and replied, "I'm not sure you still have a job you obnoxious little turd! Who do you think you are?"

Collin replied, "But my Dad promised me.."

Ron cut him off again and replied, "You don't work for your Daddy and I'll be dammed if I'm going to let you abuse my customers, machines or techs, understand!"

Collin didn't say anything more but got up and left the room.

Ron got up, looked out of his window and thought, "I'm starting to hate this job again, why am I always the one to get these butt holes?"

He noticed his building buddy waving to him from across the street, Ron could tell she was wearing a very short and risqué outfit. He returned the wave and she picked up a large piece of paper that read, "Lunch?"

Ron was caught by surprise, his first instinct was to say, "Hell yes!"

Then he quickly thought, "I can't do that, I'm married," and quickly scribbled on a piece of paper, "I'm married!"

She scribbled, "So!" and held it up to the window.

He thought to himself, "Oh man, this is a single man's dream!"

He scribbled, "I'm flattered but I can't."

She held up a sign that read, "That's too bad," and walked away.

He continued staring out of his window, almost in shock and thought, "Did that just happen? New York women can't be that easy."

He sat back down at his desk and thought out loud, "Goose Poopies!"

Mike finally arrived in the city just as Renee was calling him to take a call at a copy shop on the east side. He explained that he had to finish up at A Force of one and overheard Ron in the background telling her to let Mike finish up and get out of there.

Mike arrived onsite and Bruce the owner was there in the copy room with the part waiting for him.

Bruce started right in, "This part arrived over twenty minutes ago. Where were you? I expect you here first thing in the morning."

Mike looked at his watch and realized he was right on time.

Mike replied, "Bruce, I am an employee of At Your Service, I start my morning when my boss tells me to, not you," and waited for a response.

Bruce was livid but knew Mike was right. He threw the part on a table next to the machine, put both hands on his hips and yelled out in a somewhat feminine voice, "Do you know where you are, huh, do you? Do you know who you are messing with young man, huh? I always get my way and harass the hell out of anyone who dares to challenge me, do you understand, huh, do you?"

He became even more enraged when Mike slipped a little while holding back a laugh.

Bruce continued, "You think this is funny, do you, huh, get this machine fixed immediately!" then stormed out of the room.

Once Bruce left, Mike could not contain himself any longer and busted out laughing. He put his hands on his hips and mimicked Bruce's little tirade.

He then realized Gary was still in the room and Gary told Mike, "You shouldn't do that, Bruce is a really important man, you're going to be in big trouble."

Mike looked at him and replied, "Will you leave me alone? I'd be half done if you two would cut the crap and let me do my job."

Mike started pulling the machine apart and realized it needed a lot of work. It was one of Greg's old machines so Mike was getting used to this scenario.

He replaced the part and Bruce came in to personally test run the machine.

Bruce was obviously still upset and Mike couldn't help but be amused, Bruce had such a strange way about him.

Mike tried to calm the situation and told Bruce, "Please let me know if the machine gives you any other problems. I noticed some parts were worn so I'll order them and install them when they arrive."

Bruce quickly replied, "Worn parts? Which ones? I demand they be replaced immediately, my machine is to be kept at the optimal level of readiness at all times, do you understand me?"

Mike thought to himself, " Why did I tell him that?" and quickly replied, "Bruce, I feel the same way as you about that, I strive to keep my machines maintained at the highest level possible. I'll get them installed as soon as I can but the parts aren't stocked locally, I checked assuming you would prefer they be installed today."

Bruce put his hands on his hips and replied, "Just see that you do, I'll expect you here tomorrow at the latest." He turned and quickly left the room.

Mike left as quickly as he could and wondered where he should grab lunch. He had his tool cart with him and figured the downtown sales office would work. He heard a few of the guys were heading there so he grabbed a sandwich from one of the street vendors and headed over.

Ron returned to his office, he needed to get out for awhile after the run in with Collin and the encounter with his building buddy. He had decided to spend a little time with Chuck's secretary, Millie.

Ron had found Millie to be a real character and never realized until now how deathly afraid of modern technology she was. Millie went on and on about how unhealthy cell phone radiation was and how computer screens would cause cancer. Millie had a theory about how computers were a plot to take over the world and even now, the screens were really two way and someone could watch you all day from the other side. Ron noticed some books on her shelf, among them were, "Cobalt for Dummies," and, "C++ and you."

Ron asked her what she was doing with them and she replied, "They've been there almost as long as I have, I have no idea who they belonged too. They make nice paperweights though."

While on the subject of how long she had been there, Millie explained that she had started working at AYS just before Chuck came onboard. The last district manager was a very hard working and down to earth man she loved working for.

She added, "Not like this guy, he's such a fart knocker, she whispered to Ron. She added, "I'm sorry, I shouldn't use such strong language, I picked that up from one of my grandchildren."

Ron replied, "Don't worry Mildred, I've called him much worse than that."

It was then that Ron developed a strong liking for Mildred, she reminded him of his sweet aunt Mary, the one who used to bake him fresh cookies when he was a boy.

Mildred continued, "I don't know how or why but for some reason, Chuck just showed up one day, unannounced and took over. I'm just biding my time, I'll be retiring soon I hope. My husband just retired a couple of years ago and I can't wait to join him Ron."

Chuck had returned so Millie had to get back to work. Ron returned to his office and found Collin sitting in his chair, looking at the latest spreadsheet that Ron had left behind.

Ron told him, "What are you doing here and get the hell out of my seat!"

Collin started to respond and told Ron, "I talked to my Dad, he told me not to worry."

Chuck barged in and told Ron, "We need to speak, in private."

They both looked at Collin who responded, "Go on, I'll wait."

Ron replied, "Excuse me, get out of my office, now!"

After Collin left the office, Chuck explained, "I received a call from one of our Vice Presidents at the home office. He advised me that we are to take care of Collin, no matter what."

Ron replied, "What, that punk is lucky I haven't planted my foot up his butt yet, are you crazy!"

Chuck added, "Do what you need to do but he's ours now."

Ron replied, "You mean mine, this is how you ended up with a team of screwballs in the first place Chuck, this kid is going to be nothing but trouble!"

Chuck replied, "Like I always say Ron, when the going gets rough, the.."

Ron cut him off and finished the sentence, "The district manager say's see ya, right Chuck!"

Chuck looked confused and responded, "There's nothing we can do about it Ron, deal with him."

As Chuck left Ron's office, Ron sat back and wondered, "How am I going to get rid of this kid?"

He called Collin back into his office and got on the phone with Greg. He explained to Greg, "I'm sending you one of our new techs, right out of training. I want you to show him the ropes."

After giving Greg's phone number and present location to Collin, Collin advised Ron that he had been looking at the spreadsheet on his desk. He noticed all the parts data was routed through the same location except for one and that one location was substantially higher than the rest.

Ron replied, "So you like stuff like that, number crunching, data and spreadsheets?"

Collin admitted, "It's always been a passion of mine, statistical analysis and number crunching."

Ron asked, "Why aren't you working in that field?"

Collin replied, "I did for awhile but my coworkers were all butt holes."

Ron quickly replied, "Are you starting to see a pattern here Collin, it seems that no matter where you go, everyone else is a butt hole, are you sure it's not you?"

Collin thought about it briefly and replied, "No, it's them."

Ron shook his head and responded, "Never mind, I guess you better get going, Greg will be waiting for you."

After Collin left, Ron looked at the spreadsheet again and noticed the sequence of I.P. address locations Collin had pointed out. He thought out loud, "I'll be dammed, the little turd is right."

He noticed the address always appeared at night and usually had a large number attached to it. Ron got up and headed to see Rob, the regional specialist. Rob was much like Al only responsible for the entire region instead of Ron's team. He was also the technical coordinator with the main office. Rob might shed some light on the unexpected number.

At the Sales office, Mike arrived to find Brad and John eating lunch in one of the cubicles, Joyce was there and looked upset about something. Everyone was unusually quiet so Mike asked, "Where's the funeral?"

John replied, "I was just at Investco, they were wheeling in one of Titans new copiers."

Brad cut in and said he had seen Lyzette, the sales rep from Titan there last week. He alerted Joyce at the time but apparently it was too late. Joyce met with Oscar, her main contact at Investco but he seemed completely uninterested.

John added, "It makes sense now."

Just then Ivanna, a senior sales rep of At Your Service came in. Ivanna was Joyce's team leader and had been known to be a pit bull when a potential sale was looming. Still in her mid thirties, in great shape and very attractive, she was made team leader for a reason, she lived for a fight.

Ivanna overheard some of what the others were talking about and asked for the details. As soon as Joyce mentioned Lyzette she said, "Say no more, I've had dealings with Lyzette before. It wouldn't be the first time she's made a sale on her back."

John looked at Joyce and with his heavy Brooklyn accent said, "You better get busy with Oscar Joyce," with a chuckle. They all started laughing but stopped when they saw the hurt look on Joyce's face.

Ivanna turned it around, looked at John and gave him a light smack on the butt, then winced in pain and said, "Damn, a girl could break a nail on that thing."

John replied, "I put a lot into that butt," not immediately realizing how it sounded.

Everyone busted out laughing and Brad tried to add, "He means he works it out in the gym a lot," and realized his response didn't sound any better.

By now Joyce was laughing so hard she had tears in her eyes and added as best as she could, "Come on John, Oscar may swing both ways, can't you take one for the team?"

Ivanna changed the subject slightly and shared with them a story about Lyzette from her first encounter with her.

Ivanna went on, "Lyzette's real name is Abigail Frumpmeyer or flabby Abby as she used to be called during her childhood. She is certifiably crazy, when Lyzette was growing up her Mother used to enter her sister in these beauty pageants. You know, the one's for five year olds. As a result I hear Lyzette was ignored a lot and eventually became very jealous of her sister. Instead of being like her sister she vowed to become a successful business woman instead of a beauty queen.

Joyce replied, "There's nothing wrong with that."

Ivanna added, That's not all my dear, Lyzette is a dreamer, high on image and ambition but severely lacking in brains. She eventually realized she wasn't cut out to be a business woman, not a good one anyway. That's when she started resorting to screwing her way to the top. I have to imagine she's not very good at that either, after all, she's never become anything more than a half assed sales rep.

One more thing and I've seen this myself, "In her briefcase she used to keep these old, decrepit Barbie doll's, one looked like a business woman Barbie or something and the other was a beauty pageant Barbie. I was in a club one night and Lyzette was there, all alone in a booth making these voices. I snuck up behind and watched her carry on this weird conversation with the Barbie dolls, she really is scary."

After a moment of complete silence, John was the first to respond and said, "Wow, is this turning anyone else on besides me?"

Brad added, "You're sick dude, that's the kind of girl you sleep with and never wake up again."

Joyce responded, "Are we sure we want to mess with her?"

Ivanna looked at Joyce and replied, "Honey, I hope you have the stomach for a fight, this could get nasty, might be fun too! Let me think about this tonight, in the meantime we need details. Spend as much time at Investco as you can without raising suspicion."

John had a call at Fusia so they worked it out with Renee that Mike would take the Fusia call. Brad and John would head to Investco and start gathering as much information as possible.

Brad and John arrived at Investco just as a heated discussion was starting. Oscar had just closed his office door and Lyzette was with him. The key operators were upset and just starting to voice their frustrations about the new Titan equipment. John and Brad had arrived at the perfect time. Apparently Lyzette had been showing up a lot over the last month. One of the operators said he saw Oscar and Lyzette on the train coming in together in the morning, more than once.

One of the operators looked at Brad and said, "We don't want to lose you guys, the Titan techs are all butt holes."

Another operator added, "And their machine is horrible, it constantly jams, you tell their techs about it and all they say is it's the paper we're running through it."

Then, Oscars door opened and out came Lyzette. She was actually attractive with blond hair and a nice shape, but she almost always appeared neurotic which wiped away any attraction to her for most men.

Her eyes locked on John's and the wry smile she was wearing quickly disappeared.

She said, "What are you two doing here, spying or saying goodbye to your little friends?" pointing at the AYS machines.

John replied, "You mean the ones that actually work."

At that, one of the operators let out a chuckle while the others remained perfectly quiet. Lyzette had a scary look on her face.

She responded, "It won't be much longer, the next time I see you you'll be wheeling those piece of crap machines out of here."

Oscar came out just as she finished speaking and Brad, who was closest to them
overheard him whisper in Lyzette's ear, "Shh, this has to be kept quiet for now."

Oscar spoke up and told her, "Look at the time, we better be getting out of here," and sheepishly started moving Lyzette out of the room.

They all heard Lyzette give a loud sickly laugh on the way out.

Brad said, "Holy crap, did you hear that, there's something seriously wrong with that woman."

John looked at Brad, held his finger straight out and replied, "Brad, remember what I said before about her turning me on," then let his finger go limp and added, "Forget that, she's freaking crazy!"

After Oscar and Lyzette left, the operators started voicing their feelings again. One commented, "She's got Oscar wrapped around her finger."

John replied, "We call it whipped, and not around her finger."

One of the operators added, "Oscar hasn't been himself lately, every time Lyzette is around he gets goofy."

Brad replied, "Like a guy in love."

John added, "More like a guy who's getting some."

They all started laughing but then stopped when they remembered that sickly laugh, one of the operators said, "Poor Oscar."

Brad asked, "What did she mean, we'll be wheeling our machines out of here soon?"

One of the operators replied, "I overheard Oscar talking to Lyzette about a big demo coming up at Titan, they must be planning to take over the copy center."

Brad and John looked at one another and thought, that would be a disaster. AYS has a lot of equipment here and it brought in lots of revenue.

As they were leaving, they asked the operators to call them if they heard anything else, especially any dates for a demo.

In the mean time, Mike had just arrived at Fusia and was excited. He had never been there before and had heard lots of great things about the account. He stepped off of the elevator and was amazed. It resembled a nightclub more than a business. The place was dimly lit and had a crystal ball on the ceiling with lights pointed at it, as it spun it cast rays of light everywhere. There was dance music coming through the loudspeakers and Al was right, every woman he saw was a perfect ten.

He made his way to the receptionist's desk and introduced himself as Mike, the copier tech from At Your Service.

The receptionist replied in a heavy British accent, "Hello Mike, the copier tech from at your service, I'm Kandi, the guest welcoming coordinator from Fusia," almost seeming to mock him.

Mike asked about the British accent and where in Britain she was from, she responded somewhat coldly, "I'm actually from Australia if you must know, Melbourne to be precise."

Mike apologized for the mistake but Kandi couldn't care less and told him, "Alright then, lets get you to Jordan."

She picked up the phone and waited a few seconds, then spoke and said, "Jordan, I see your copier is down again, you have Mike the tech from at your service here in front of me, please hurry dear."

Mike said nothing, he realized Kandi was stuck up so he concentrated on the job at hand. After what seemed like the longest minute had gone by, Jordan came out and escorted him to the copier.

Kandi said nothing, but had a look that suggested she was waiting for a thank you from Mike.

Jordan welcomed Mike and said, "I'm so glad you're here, I have two machines and a lot of work to do. With one machine down it's ruining my day."

As Mike was passing Kandi he made it a point to thank Jordan for coming out so quickly and said nothing to Kandi, he thought he heard a disapproving noise like "Hmmm," coming from Kandi's direction and thought, "Good, I got her."

Jordan was a small, petite girl in her early twenties. She had long black hair and being surrounded by women who were perfect tens probably took away from her beauty. But she was actually a very attractive girl and very personable, unlike the receptionist. Then Mike realized this was the girl Brad liked so much and thought, "He has great taste."

Mike and Jordan talked on the way to the copy room. She admitted she hated the people here at Fusia and added, "They're all so phony. You'll see what I mean when you've been here a few times but don't believe anything these people tell you. They're all trying to impress each other and will stab you in the back in a heart beat."

They arrived at the copier and Jordan showed Mike a very slight distortion in a copy of someone's face she was printing.

Mike admitted he couldn't see the distortion.

Jordan laughed and said, "You sound like Brad, do they train you guys to not see stuff."

Mike opened his tool bag and pulled out a magnifying glass, looked again and said, "Damn Jordan, you're right, how the hell did you see that?"

He got started trying to track down what was causing the problem, Brad was keeping the machine in such great shape there were no worn parts.

Mike thought he was going to end up with whiplash, every few minutes a secretary would come into the copy room and he'd turn his head to look at who it was, each one was more beautiful than the other.

At one point, Jordan threw a balled up piece of paper at him just as he was turning his head again, nailing him right between the eyes. She laughed and said, "Got ya, all you guys are the same, you can't take your eyes off these girls, what is it?"

Mike replied, "I guess you didn't catch me yet, I've looked at you a few times too. I hope you know you've got all these girls beat."

Jordan smiled and didn't say anything.

Mike wondered how anyone could concentrate on fixing the machine with so many distractions. After a couple of hours of searching, Mike found a bearing that was slightly bound up, he lubricated the bearing and finally the copies came out looking great again.

Jordan thanked Mike for helping her out of a jam and Mike replied, "I wish all of our customers were like you Jordan. It's nice to be appreciated once in awhile."

She replied, "Believe me, I know the feeling, this place sucks."

Mike added, "I don't know if it helps much but Brad is always singing your praises to the rest of us, he's always telling us how great you are."

Mike thought he saw Jordan start blushing and she replied, "He does, that's sweet."

Mike thought to himself, "These two have to get together."

He was just cleaning up when Renee called him, A Force of One placed a call, something about installing some parts. He thought to himself, "Damn," and told Renee not to worry, he'd take care of it.

He packed his tools and headed for the elevator, passing Kandi along the way. He said goodbye and was going to say nice meeting you but decided to wait until she responded. She didn't look up or say anything so Mike got on the elevator and left.

Once on the street, he called Bruce and told him, "It wasn't necessary to place a call, I haven't forgotten our appointment but it's not a problem that you did."

Bruce replied, "I have a service contract with you guys and place calls whenever I want."

Mike left it at that, realizing he needed to find a way to get Bruce under control, but that would come another day, hopefully soon.

He told Bruce, "I'll install the parts when they arrive, again there's no need to place another call, we now have one in the system." Mike knew Bruce would just ignore him and place calls all day anyway. He ordered a couple of the many parts he knew he would need and arranged for a morning delivery, then thought, "I'll never tell Bruce anything again."

It was just about quitting time so he called Brad to see how he had made out at Investco, they were going to meet at the sales office in the morning so Mike planned to start his day there, then after a long day he went home.

The next day, Mike met up with Brad and John at the sales office as planned, Joyce and Ivanna were there as well.

Bruce was already starting his every twenty minute call routine. Mike told Renee he would take care of Bruce and wondered what the tool number was for handcuffs and a muzzle.

John told Mike, "Bruce is the kind of guy you just want to smack a few times to wake him up, make him pay a price for being a butt hole."

Mike thought for a second and replied, "Thanks, you gave me an idea John, your right, he has to pay a price."

Ivanna couldn't care less about Bruce so she started asking what Brad and John had learned about Investco. They explained that Oscar was wrapped around Lyzette's finger.

Joyce added, "That moron has no idea what he's doing, once Titan takes over they get rid of everyone and put their own people in, they run everything. Oscar will be out of a job in a month."

Brad explained that he overheard Oscar whisper to Lyzette about keeping quiet for now, she said something about the next time she saw us we'd be wheeling our machines out of there."

John added that one of the operators overheard Oscar and Lyzette talking about a big demo coming up.

Ivanna told them not to sweat too hard yet, she was going to pull in a favor but desperately needed to know when the big demo would be.

Mike recalled a conversation he had with Gertie once. Apparently she and Albert, the lobby security guard were close, as in dating from time to time. Anyone entering the building had to go through him, he would have to be the first to know about any upcoming demos.

Mike, Brad and John rushed through the sales floor, the AYS lobby and stopped at Gertie's desk. Fortunately she was there and calmly asked them, "To what do I owe the pleasure of a visit from three handsome young men?"

Although they were still out of breath from running so hard they couldn't contain themselves and all tried talking at the same time.

She laughed and said, "Calm down boys, Brad, why don't you start."

Brad started explaining what was going on at Investco and that they were planning a big demo at Titan. He added that he had heard through the grapevine that she and Albert were good friends and asked if she would talk to Albert to see if he might know when Investco would be coming in.

Gertie looked directly at Mike and said, "Heard through the grapevine hmm."

With a cute smile she added, "So you want me to use a friend, involve him in something underhanded, for our personal gain."

The boys just replied, "Please, please, please."

She added, "So what's in it for Albert and I?"

Mike responded, "I'm sure Ivanna will come up with something, this is big."

Gertie added, "I know Albert absolutely loathes Lyzette, if he can help I'm sure he will, let me see what I can do."

They stepped away from Gertie's desk saying, "Thank you, thank you, we love you Gertie."

Just then, Mikes phone went off, it was Renee and Mike knew that Bruce had probably called again. He thought to himself, "Only twice so far," then told the guy's he would catch up with them later at Rosie's but had to deal with Bruce.

Mike called Bruce, who of course was freaking out by now.

Bruce shouted into the phone, "Where are you, I told you to be here first thing in the morning, didn't I, huh, didn't I?"

Mike first asked, "Is your machine having a problem?"

Bruce replied, "No, but that's beside the point, I told you to be here and your not, where are you?"

Mike replied, "I am taking care of a critical situation, your machine is running at the moment, I'll be there as soon as possible."

With that, he grabbed a newspaper, walked to a park, sat on the first bench he could find and relaxed.

Renee called him every twenty minutes and Mike told her, "No problem, I'm dealing with Bruce right now, just text me each time he calls if you want."

Each time Bruce called, Mike would call him back and kept making him wait.

While Mike was waiting he took in the beautiful sunny day. He was really starting to appreciate New York's diversity, there were people of every race and culture passing by, each with their own unique way about them. Many of them were pretty comical to watch while others, like some of the secretary's were absolutely gorgeous.

He looked around the park and noticed three people sitting on a bench sunning themselves. One of them lowered their mirror long enough for Mike to tell it was the three smucks from Bill's team. Mike shook his head and thought out loud, "I guess some people just know how to live."

As he continued glancing around, he saw Frank and Tom, walking together and watched as they made their way into a building across the street from the park. He thought it was odd considering Tom was fired and wondered what Tom was doing in the area with Frank.

He headed over to the building entrance and saw them coming out of the building. Mike quickly turned, leaned against the building and raised the newspaper to cover his face. Neither Tom or Frank saw him and Mike observed they were both carrying AYS parts. Mike also overheard them talking about which one would take a call somewhere but he couldn't catch just where.

He then felt his phone vibrate and realized he had missed a few text messages from Renee, A Force of One had called again and again. Mike made note of the address, called Renee and Bruce then started heading to A Force of One.

When he got there, Gary told Mike he had never seen Bruce this upset and with that, Bruce entered the room. Mike thought he saw the veins of Bruce's head popping out as Bruce started his tirade.

"Where the hell have you been?" Bruce yelled and put both hands on his hips.

He continued, "I told you to be here first thing this morning, did I not make myself perfectly clear when you left here yesterday?"

By now Bruce's voice was breaking and he was becoming very emotional. He continued, "I kept track of every call I made this morning, look at this," then threw a sheet of paper at Mike that highlighted every call he had made.

Mike caught the paper in mid air and replied as professionally as possible, "First of all, I never said I'd be here first thing this morning nor did you say I had to be here first thing this morning. Second, your machine is running and requires normal, routine maintenance, if you read your contract you'll see maintenance is done when it's mutually convenient. Third and most important Bruce is this, every time you call me, are you aware that a dispatcher has to pick up the phone, enter your call into the system, call me and wait for me to call her back. Then I have to stop what I'm doing, get on the phone, call you, listen to you blow a gasket for ten minutes, pick up my screwdriver and figure out where I was at before I had to stop what I was doing to call you."

Mike pointed at the paper Bruce threw at him and showed him, "Look Bruce, ten calls, do you realize you took up at least three hours of our time, my time and yours, twenty minutes every time you call Bruce, twenty minutes, that's how long it takes me to respond to your call."

Bruce was upset but too emotionally drained to respond. Mike almost thought he saw a tear in Bruce's eye. Bruce just turned and walked away.

Mike turned around and caught Gary staring at him with a goofy look on his face.

Gary added, "Mike, you were wonderful, I've never seen anyone talk to Bruce like that, so macho."

Mike thought, "Oh no, now I have to deal with this guy too!"

Gary brought the parts over to Mike and daintily handed them to him.

While Mike replaced the parts, Gary stayed right behind him the whole time. At one point when Mike was leaning over, Gary was so close that Mike felt him rub up against him.

Mike shouted, "Get the hell off me you pervert, what's wrong with you, " and side stepped himself away from Gary. Gary didn't say anything but Mike noticed he was beaming.

When Mike finished installing the parts he thought it would be a good idea to talk to Bruce before he left. He knocked on Bruce's door and was called in, Bruce was just finishing a call with Ron.

Mike sat down in front of Bruce and explained, "Please understand Bruce, I'm going to do my very best to take care of your machine. I don't know what kind of service you were used to before but I am your new tech now. I'll keep your machine up and running as best as anyone can and when your machine is down I'll hustle over as quickly as possible. You're absolutely right when you say you can call as often as you want. But it really won't be necessary, in fact it just messes everything up. I promise, I'll take the best care of this account as I can."

Mike put his hand out to Bruce, who reached out and shook his hand.

Mike also never mentioned there were more parts that needed replacement but thought, "Let me get the hell out of here," he grabbed his tool cart and ran like hell to his parts drop.

Ron had called him along the way and asked, "What did you do Mike?"

You could tell Ron was holding back a laugh, and explained that Bruce was really in a tizzy. He couldn't wait to hear Mike's side of the story.

Mike explained that he couldn't take the guy anymore. Bruce was the most arrogant, obnoxious guy he had ever met so he purposefully made him wait, then blamed it on his every twenty-minute phone call routine.

Then he mentioned the operator Gary's little bump and grind, Ron couldn't hold back anymore and busted out laughing.

He added, "I'm sorry Mike. It's just that I haven't had anything to laugh about with that place in so long, it just came out, should I talk to Bruce about Gary."

Mike replied, "Not yet, it might come to that though."

Ron added, "Just don't let it get out of hand, I can nip it in the bud if needed, but for now I'll let you manage it, overall, good job. Bruce has been a pain in my ass since day one, I think you got him good."

Mike replied, "We'll see."

He quickly dropped his tool cart off at his parts drop, Roger wasn't around so he quickly headed to Rosie's.

Once there he caught up with Al, Brad and John, who had heard about his adventure at A Force of One.

Al was the first to lay into Mike and said, "I heard you made a new friend today. How's your buddy Gary doing? Did you order him flowers yet?" They all laughed and Al added, "I hear you really got to Bruce though, the best part was it was by the book, I haven't heard Ron so happy in a long time."

Mike replied, "I'm so sick of being henpecked by Bruce. Who the hell does he think he is?" Mike put his hands on his hips and mimicked Bruce, they all laughed and Al added, "Nuckin Fut's."

Mike mentioned to Brad about the call he took for him at Fusia. "Jordan is so sweet, if you don't make a move on her soon, I might."

Brad was in the middle of drinking his beer and almost choked when Mike told him that.

Brad replied, "Come on Mike, what do you want all the action? You already have Gary, maybe Bruce too."

The guys were laughing as Ivanna and Joyce entered and joined them at the bar.

Ivanna asked that they move to a quieter table so they went upstairs. It wasn't a busy day so Rosie's closed the upstairs, you couldn't get more private.

Al saw Sandy the waitress sitting in a booth, filing her nails. He asked her to come upstairs and take their order. She never looked back at him but did wave her hand as if to say I heard you.

John's phone rang and everyone became quiet, hoping it was Gertie. He took out his pen and started writing as everyone listened intently. They could see him writing, "Milk, bread and condoms."

John hung up and everyone asked who it was that had called him.

John replied, "That was my Grandmother, She wants me to pick up a few things on the way home."

Ivanna responded, "Condoms, for your Grandmother?"

John replied, "What? She may be old but she's not dead yet, I guess she's like a mega milf or something!"

They all shook their heads and started comparing notes about Investco and the Titan takeover. Brad explained they were hoping to get word from Gertie or one of the Investco operators about the date of the big demo.

Just then, Brad's phone rang and this time no one became excited after the false alarm with John. However this time it was Gertie and she had heard from Albert. The big demo was Friday, tomorrow. Albert had Lyzette, Oscar and someone else meeting in the lobby at 10 a.m.

As Brad was hanging up he said, "Love you Gertie."

Everyone at the table stopped everything. Joyce and Ivanna kept asking over and over, "What did she say? When's the demo Brad? What did she say?"

Brad replied, "Something about bringing condoms," then added, "I'm just kidding!"

Brad then explained what Gertie had found out, Ivanna called downstairs and asked where Sandy was, Ivanna was ready for a drink.

They started working on a plan and Ivanna explained that she was calling in a favor from an old friend at Investco. Back in the day it was Ivanna and her now Vice President friend who placed the first AYS machines at Investco. She explained she would get her friend to meet her in the AYS demo room. If we can keep Oscar and Lyzette from getting to the showroom and get Albert to detain Lyzette's contact we may have a shot at stopping this.

Robin arrived upstairs and everyone asked where the hell Sandy was, they asked her to come up at least ten minutes ago.

Robin replied, "You're kidding right, you think she's going to come all the way up here. Princess Sandy is still downstairs doing her nails. What the hell are you guys doing up here anyway? This section is closed tonight!"

Ivanna gave her a twenty dollar tip and Robin added, "Never mind, what do you need"

A few minutes later, Robin brought them their drinks and told them, "Yell if you need me," as she headed back downstairs. They overheard her tell Sandy, "Hey, you lazy bitch, let me explain you're job description, when customers want a drink, you get off of your fat ass and bring them a drink!"

Al responded, "You think Greg and Sandy are twins separated at birth?"

Ivanna continued, "Joyce, I'll need you to meet with Lyzette's contact in the lobby and somehow get him to our showroom instead of Titans, can I count on you?"

Joyce chugged her drink, a wine spritzer and let out a loud, "Whooo yahh! "
This was so out of character for Joyce and they all cracked up laughing.

Joyce looked at Ivanna and in a very serious voice said, "Let's screw that bitch."

Ivanna replied, "That's my girl."

The day of the demo was upon them, it was dress down Friday, their second one and they didn't look like techs today.

Brad, Mike and John let Ron and Renee in on what they were doing. Ron admitted he was proud of their effort but advised them he might have to protect AYS interests and wash his hands of the whole thing if they were caught. He did however arrange to borrow a few techs from other areas to help cover their calls.

First thing in the morning, Brad and John met at Investco, had one of the operators place a call and log a problem with one of the machines.

Mike remained outside and kept watch, It wasn't long before he spotted Oscar and Lyzette heading into the building and alerted Brad.

Brad and John ducked behind the machine as if they were troubleshooting something so Lyzette and Oscar wouldn't see them. A few minutes later, Lyzette and Oscar entered the copy center and headed into Oscars office.

Brad and John approached the office door and overheard Lyzette tell Oscar how hot and excited this whole thing made her. She added, "If everything goes as planned today, I'm going to make you the happiest man alive tonight."

John whispered to Brad, "Ewwwwhhh, could you imagine that, with her?"

Lyzette said to Oscar, "What was that? I heard something."

Oscar replied, "Don't worry, it was probably one of the operators coming in."

Brad got to work on Oscars door lock and stuffed the keyhole with a large paper clip, then made sure it was locked tight. John disconnected Oscar's phone and then they waited. After twenty minutes went by they heard the door handle rattle, Oscar was trying to open the door.

Brad and John overheard Lyzette tell Oscar, "Get out of my way you fool, can't you even open a door."

Lyzette gave it a solid turn, then a pull that made the door rattle hard.

John told Brad, "She's strong."

Then she started really going off.

Brad replied, "I hope she took her meds today," then heard a really loud thud.

John responded, "Nope, I guess not."

The noise they heard was Oscar being thrown against the door.

In the meantime, Lyzette's contact had just arrived in the lobby of the building and Albert alerted Gertie, who alerted Joyce. Like clockwork, Joyce met Oscar's contact and brought him up to Ivanna who already had her contact in the demo room.

Ivanna explained some of the details of what was going on between Lyzette and Oscar. Oscar's contact was actually not too surprised and had heard some bad stories about Titan.

Ivanna's VP friend explained that AYS had always been a great partner with Investco, although he was a VP he wasn't there to tell anyone in the copy center or purchasing dept. who to do business with, as long as it was on the up and up.

With that, Lyzette's contact mentioned he was a little upset that Lyzette and Oscar hadn't called or met him in the lobby, "You wouldn't know anything about that, would you?" he asked Joyce.

Joyce replied, "No, but I'll chalk it up as our good fortune," and turned their attention to the new equipment they were selling.

Back at Investco, Brad, John and Mike, who finally joined them, were enjoying the show. By now the key operators were all at work, listening to Lyzette berate Oscar. They kind of felt sorry for him but knew he had put all their jobs at risk. With Oscars phone disconnected, no cell phone coverage in the copy center, everything was going as planned.

They heard a couple of loud crashes in Oscar's office when suddenly a filing cabinet came crashing through Oscars wall. It just missed one of the operators and crashed into the copier that Titan had installed.

Lyzette came out through the newly formed opening first, followed by Oscar.

Lyzette was wide eyed and angry, scary angry. They quickly ducked behind the machine again and heard her yell at Oscar, "If we miss that demo you're a dead man."

Oscar and Lyzette left in a hurry while Mike found a working phone and called Joyce. Ivanna was showing the equipment, so Joyce was able to pick up her phone. He advised her that Lyzette and Oscar had escaped and were on their way back. Joyce told them not to worry, the demo was going well and it would be some time before they would be leaving, then thanked the boys for all their help.

They called Renee and told her, "Mission complete."

Renee quickly replied, "Good, are you guys ready to get off your butts? Stu's area is backed up, we haven't heard from him all morning." This was unlike Stu, he was lazy but usually did his job and responded to Renee's calls, just very slowly.

Brad, John and Mike split up and took care of Stu's calls. When they were done it was late in the day so they met at Rosie's.

Joyce and Ivanna were already there, sitting at the bar and as happy as could be. They hugged and thanked the boys for all their work. Ivanna ordered the first round and told Bert to keep them coming.

Mike asked Ivanna, "So I guess things went well."

Ivanna replied, "Unbelievably well."

Joyce cut in, "We're upgrading half of the fleet, that's twenty machines, all with five year contracts," she looked at Ivanna and added, "Sorry, I'm just so excited."

Ivanna gave her a hug and told her, "That's alright, you should be excited, this is big."

Ivanna picked up her shot of tequila and raised it in a toast, "To teamwork," and downed her shot, they all raised their glasses and downed their shots. Joyce gave one of her, "Whooo yahhs!" You couldn't help but laugh when she did that, it just wasn't what you would expect to hear from her.

As they were celebrating, Ron, Al and Stu suddenly appeared behind them.

Their mood wasn't quite as festive as the others so John asked, "What happened Boss, your Viagra get lost in the mail?"

They laughed and Ron shot back, "No, but Renee got a message from the he man sex shop in the village, your leather cat suit is almost ready but the custom butt flap you requested got stuck, its delaying the shipment."

They all busted out laughing, Joyce was laughing so hard she had tears in her eyes and Ivanna high fived Ron and said, "That's why you're the big dog."

Ron added, "Stu, you want to say anything,"

Stu replied, "Yeah, lets order some more shots, I'm thirsty."

Al explained, "We Just bailed our buddy Stu here out of out of the midtown precinct."

Ron added, "Remember what I said about dress down Friday's?"

They looked at Stu and realized he was dressed in a black, wrinkled jumpsuit with sneakers.

Al continued, "Apparently one of our customers mistook Stu for a homeless guy, sleeping behind the machine."

Stu started defending himself right away, "The customer's a butt hole, how can a homeless guy get in with their security, they placed a call, they should have known a tech would be behind their machine, I'm never going back there again."

After the barrage, Stu looked up at everyone with a slight smirk, everyone looked at him and Stu added, "What?"

They just shook their heads.

By now, the shooter girl Amanda made it over to the group and with the hottest Spanish accent said, "Come on people, its Friday, liven it up here."

She put her mixing cup on the bar and placed both hands on her holster, one hand pulled out the tequila bottle, the other a bottle of her shooter concoction.
She drew and poured both into her mixing cup, sealed the cup and shook it vigorously.
She let out a loud, " ay, ay, ay, ay, ay, ay, ay, ay !! " then smashed it on the bar and
added, "Who's first?"

Stu started it off and it continued after that, Amanda must have spent an hour at the bar with the AYS crew. She had such a friendly way about her and was a natural flirt. Between her personality, her incredible looks and the shooter girl outfit it was difficult to turn her down.

Kelly arrived after awhile and got in a couple of shots followed by Renee and a few other dispatchers. It had turned into an all out party in no time.

Mike was talking to Ron and Brad about his call at A Force of one when he noticed the receptionist Kandi from Fusia seated at one of the tables. She was out with a few of her girl friends and looked like she was having a good time.

Mike pointed her out to Brad and Ron, then told them, "I have to go over there."

Brad quickly replied, "She's like the ice queen Mike, forget her."

Ron added, "Come on Mike, what about Gary and Bruce, you'll break their hearts."

Mike responded, "If she's drinking maybe she'll lighten up, if nothing else I just want to rattle her cage a little."

Mike headed over just as the table behind Kandi's was opening up. He took a seat without Kandi noticing and listened for an opportunity to cut in. He waited for that heavy Australian accent but never heard it. Mike turned around and realized she was speaking in a normal voice, with no accent.

One of her friends looked at Mike and motioned to Kandi with her eyes that they had company. Kandi turned around and Mike said, "Hi Kandi, it's Mike the tech from At Your Service, are you still Kandi, the guest welcoming coordinator from Australia, Melbourne to be precise," and flashed a huge grin.

She looked at Mike and had such an embarrassed look on her face. She replied with the Australian accent, "Just trying to lock in an American accent for a part I'm trying out for if you must know."

Then one of her girl friends, who had a little too much to drink busted out laughing and said, "Give it up Kandi, talk to the guy, he's cute."

Kandi rolled her eyes and said, "Alright, I'm really from Philadelphia, nothing personal Mike but everyone at Fusia puts on a phony persona, they demand it."

Mike told her, "Let's start over and forget the phony crap."

After a couple of minutes of conversation, John and a couple of other techs came over and started talking to the other girls at the table.

Brad was still at the bar with Joyce and Ivanna and asked about how she would repay Gertie and Albert for their help in all of this.

Ivanna replied, "I'm taking really good care of them tonight."

As we speak they're enjoying a night on the town. Dinner, a show and a night at the Waldorf. We couldn't have done any of this without them."

Ron was standing at the top of the stairs with Al, looking down at all that was going on at Rosie's and admitted, I'm really starting to like this job.

Al replied, "Our crew is starting to come together, I think we have something special going on here!"

Chapter 7 - Love and Logic

Ron was in his office waiting for Rob, the regional specialist and Al to arrive. They were going to compare notes about the parts numbers and rogue IP address situation.

He looked out of his window and noticed his building buddy across the street, waving to him again. Ron waved back and thought, "Is that all this girl does all day, must be nice."

Today she was wearing a very tight, short and low cut red dress. Ron thought to himself, "Be strong!"

She held up a sign again that read, "Lunch later?"

Ron shook his head, quickly made up a sign that read, "I still can't, I'm married."

She held up another sign that read, "What's your phone number?"

Ron thought to himself, "Poor thing, she must really be hot for me and held his sign up again, the one that said, I can't, I'm married."

He thought, "Maybe I should meet her, just to say hello and let her know I'm flattered. I don't want to hurt her feelings or anything. Maybe I should talk to Angela and see if she wouldn't mind."

Ron didn't realize it but he was not the only person that his building buddy was flashing her signs at. There were at least two other men and one woman in Ron's building who were showing an interest.

Ron thought, "Let me talk to Angela, maybe she'll sympathize, I wouldn't want to leave the girl feeling completely rejected."

Just then, Al and Rob knocked on the door and entered. Rob said he was sorry for the delay, he was just putting the finishing touches on the fix for the new software.

Al added, "Amen, that new software is a nightmare!"

Ron stepped away from his window, went to his desk and showed them a number on a spreadsheet, then another page of his own calculations.

Rob looked at Ron's numbers and added, "They match up pretty well with mine, these numbers are alarming to put it mildly."

Ron added, "So where are we losing these parts?"

Rob held up a spreadsheet and replied, "Look at this IP address, I see a lot of activity here. Do you notice that it's very similar to the corporate IP address on our network? I narrowed its location to an office somewhere in midtown, I can't pinpoint it just yet though."

Al added, "You know, Mike mentioned seeing Frank and Tom together last week, carrying parts. I think he said it was in the midtown area too."

Ron asked Rob, "Do you think we can get a more accurate fix on the location?"

Rob replied, "Given enough time, absolutely."

Just then, Al's phone rang, it was Renee. Apparently a machine at Investco that Greg and Collin were working on caught fire and Al was needed there immediately.

Ron shook his head and added, "Never a dull moment."

Rob responded, "It's almost impossible for that to happen, do you know how many safety features are designed into these machines to prevent that!"

Ron replied, "Al, let me know if Collin had anything to do with this, I'll call Mike and get more information about Tom and Frank."

Rob excused himself and Ron headed to Chuck's office to bring him up to date.

When Al arrived onsite, he could smell the charred electronics as soon as he got off of the elevator. He was expecting an assault from Oscar as soon as he arrived but his assistant Chris greeted him instead.

Chris pulled Al aside and told him, "I don't know what you have to do but we never want to see those two techs in here again, understand! They almost started a fire, the whole floor had to be evacuated. We can't have this Al, we used to tolerate Greg but this new guy is off the wall. He's obnoxious and pushy, he's got to go!

Al replied, "No problem Chris, let me get to the bottom of this and figure out what went wrong, I promise I'll take care of this."

Chris walked Al into the main copy room and Collin was the first to greet him.

Collin explained, "I don't know what happened Al, I rewired one circuit board as a favor, trying to get the machine to run for them and then it smoked."

Al pulled Collin to the side and told him, "Collin, what are doing redesigning machines, especially circuit board's, we never do that in the field, what's wrong with you!"

Collin quickly replied, "You sound just like my lame instructor, what's wrong with you! I checked the wall power, this customer is running his wall power two volts too high, that was probably why it smoked."

Al shot back, "The machine is designed to run fine even if the power is ten volt's too high."

Collin replied, "But not with the change I made!"

Al got right in Collin's face and told him, "That's why we don't redesign machine's in the field, get it!"

Collin's face turned red and he was obviously becoming angry with Al, in his entire life he had never learned to accept that he could be wrong, about anything.

Al then approached Greg and asked what had happened, Greg admitted he didn't know, Collin grabbed the circuit board from his hand's, came back with it a few minute's later and here we are."

As Al surveyed the damage he could see a section of wiring harness that had smoked. He took off his jacket and started troubleshooting the mess.

Mike was just finishing up a call at SafeTnet insurance. Carl was having a problem with his stapling unit but it was nothing major. After Mike had gotten used to the account he had confirmed his suspicions about Carl. Carl had a reputation for damaging his machine on purpose to get out of work. Mike had determined it was more a problem with Carl's hand's being so large and strong that he easily damaged any plastic parts he had to handle. In this case, Carl had tried to load staple wire and bent the tip of the cartridge, a cheap plastic part. Add to that his last tech was Greg, who let the machine go to hell and the account was a disaster.

Since taking over the account Mike had completely rebuilt the machine and worked with Carl as best he could. Carl was still a challenge however, he still had a bad temper he struggled to keep under control and was a little impatient at times. Mike had developed as good a rapport as anyone could and now the account was at least manageable.

Carl came back into the copy room just as Mike was finishing up. One of Carl's customers was coming in just as Carl was coming out and rang the annoying bell at the front entrance. Nothing happened and the woman yelled out, "What's wrong with this thing?"

Mike looked at Carl, Carl smiled and Mike responded, "You're welcome Carl."

Mike had rigged the bell for Carl a few weeks earlier, which helped put Mike on Carl's good side.

After helping his customer, Carl joined Mike at the machine. Mike joked and told him, "Alright Carl, it's fixed, you know the drill, I get a five minute head start before you try to run it, right."

Carl smiled slightly and told Mike, "Thanks, I think."

Those words meant a lot from Carl, Mike recalled how it used to be at SafeTnet when he first started. Carl used to be scary and no one wanted to come here. Now his entire territory was transformed, he had worked his butt off cleaning up Greg's messes and was now starting to enjoy the results.

Just as Mike was leaving his phone rang, it was Renee. He picked up the phone and told her, "Are you going to talk dirty to me again?

Renee replied, "No wise ass, you ready to do some work for me?"

Mike replied, "Oh come on, please, not even a little?"

Renee went on and told Mike it was getting unusually busy and asked if he could take a call in John's territory. The new software that was installed on some of the machines was having problems, it was tying everyone up. The machines would just lockup and require frequent reboots. Mike's machine at A Force of One was one of them and Bruce was driving him nuts over it. Ron finally had to step in and promised Bruce he would be the first to get the fix when it became available.

Mike told Renee, "No problem, I'm free right now, "So she dispatched him to Nature's copy, the copy center in the village Mike had been to once before.

Renee added in a very sexy voice, "Now go get dirty for me my little boy toy!," then breathed deeply into the phone and hung up. Just before she hung up Mike overheard a couple of the dispatchers let out a loud laugh.

Mike thought to himself, "Sometimes I love this job!"

He started making his way to Natures copy, it had been a beautiful day earlier but now it was starting to turn very dark and cloudy. He made it half way to Natures copy when all of a sudden the sky opened up. Mike took out his umbrella and continued his walk but in no time it turned into a serious wind driven rainstorm. He didn't realize the streets were starting to flood and as he stepped off a curb, Mike planted his foot into a deep puddle and immediately felt his foot get cold and soaked. He continued but it was getting increasingly difficult, the wind whipped through the buildings in a swirling motion that blew his umbrella inside out twice.

He got to another intersection, looked up and saw Julio, the tech with the overloaded tool cart. Julio was wearing a raincoat, which now seemed to make a lot more sense than an umbrella. As Julio noticed him, he pointed to the ground in front of Mike. Mike looked down and as he did a cab rushed past him, sending a huge wave of water crashing onto him.

Mike looked up and saw Julio heading his way, as he approached him Julio told Mike, "What happened rookie, I tried to warn you, are you alright?" Julio then added, "I gave up on umbrellas years ago, look around you."

As Mike looked around he noticed there were umbrellas scattered on the ground everywhere, all blown inside out and left abandoned.

As they parted, Mike threw his umbrella to the ground in frustration and continued on his way to Natures copy. He was soaking wet and as he walked, one of his shoes squeaked every time he stepped down. He thought to himself, "I'll probably laugh about this one day," then thought again, "Nah, maybe not."

He arrived at the copy center just as the storm was letting up and the sun came out again as he opened the door. Mike looked up and thought, "Of course it clears up when I get here."

He opened the door, heard the wind chimes go off and was greeted by Bernice.

She exclaimed, "Mike, look at you, you're soaking wet, you have to get out of those clothes you poor thing!"

As she started taking off his shirt, Mike replied, "But Bernice, I can't sit here naked."

She went into the closet and pulled out a pink tie dyed bathrobe and matching slippers. Bernice handed them to Mike and told him, "I have a drier upstairs now I insist, get out of those clothes."

She again started removing Mike's shirt just as Arthur was entering the room.

Arthur shouted, "Bernie, what the hell are you doing," then pointed at Mike and added, "And you, get the hell away from my wife man!"

He let out a loud laugh and added, "I'm just kidding, you can still have her dude, you want to swap for that cute little sales girl, what's her name, Joyce?"

Mike knew Arthur was kidding but felt a stroke of jealousy run through him. He still felt a strong attraction to Joyce but was reluctant to pursue a relationship. He respected Al and his advice about office romances.

With the funky tie dyed robe on, Mike started working on the copier. It seems the machine was jamming constantly. As Mike was repairing the machine he overheard some of the customers comment about their new operator and their dress code.

Arthur responded once that Mike was one of the special needs kids they hired. He told another customer, "You know, it's not just the machine that's functionally challenged man!"

Mike finally finished working on the machine and went to the back room to wait for his clothes to dry. He still felt a slight chill so he poured a cup of Bernie's herbal tea, saw some brownies and grabbed a couple of those as well. He then sat down and finally relaxed for a while.

Artie finished working with his customer and joined Mike in the back. Mike noticed Artie was smiling and asked, "Is everything alright?"

Artie replied, "Awesome man, how do you like those brownies."

Mike responded, "You know, they have a taste I'm not familiar with but their great."

Artie added, "Bernie makes them with something extra, vanilla or nutmeg or something, I don't know, have some more dude."

Artie turned the stereo on and played some vintage Iron Butterfly, "In A Gada Da Vida." As they got into the music, Mike played air guitar while Artie played drums on a tin can he had lying around. They told jokes and Mike couldn't stop eating the brownies, he felt great.

Just then John arrived and went to the back room. He took one look at Mike and busted out laughing.

Bernice arrived just after John, noticed the brownies were almost gone along with her herbal tea. Bernice gave the cutest chuckle and said, "Artie, what did you do? You know those were my special blend brownies."

John knew what she meant and told Mike, "Stand up slowly there Mike, those things kick like a mule!"

Mike stood up but told John, "Are you kidding, I feel great!"

They all busted out laughing and Bernice explained to Mike that her special blend included Cannabis. John could tell that Mike had no idea what she was talking about so he bluntly added, "Pot, you know, Marijuana!"

At first Mike was in shock but it quickly turned to a giddy euphoria. Mike grabbed Bernice by the hand and started twirling her to the music then asked her if she had anymore.

Bernice quickly replied, "I'm sure I can whip up another batch, Artie, why don't you and John disappear for awhile and.."

John cut her off and told Mike, "Alright there Mike, I think it's time to get you out of here."

Bernie looked at John with a hurt look and added, "Killjoy, I was gonna get some."

Mike headed to the bathroom to start getting dressed but started walking and could hardly feel his feet.

Artie busted out laughing and added, "Dude, you are so wasted, you're not going to come down for hours man."

After Mike got dressed he thanked them for the great time, almost forgetting that he came there to work.

Once on the street, John looked at Mike with a grin and asked, "Should I ask how you ended up in that robe. You know you owe me big, you were almost taken advantage of by Bernice."

Mike replied, "Holy senior milf muffins, ewwww!" and busted out laughing.

Mike couldn't stop laughing about it and just about anything else they talked about.

John decided for both of them to head to Rosie's, he couldn't wait to show Mike off to the guy's. When they arrived, Mike was in a noticeably happy mood and was laughing about anything and everything.

Al, Brad and Kelly were already there and could tell that something was up with Mike. They asked and John let them in on Mike's day with Artie and Bernice. Kelly asked Mike about his bloodshot eyes and John replied, "I just rescued Mike from a fate worst than death. It was brownie day at Bernice and Arties, Mike here ate more brownies than anyone I've ever met. Were talking about Bernie's special blend brownies!"

Then asked Mike, "How you feeling there Mike?"

Mike tried to reply but he had just finished devouring the basket of nachos that were in front of him and his mouth was still full.

Then John added, "That's not the half of it, Bernice was trying to pull a fast one on Mike and get some, I do mean that literally too!"

They all busted out laughing, then Al responded first and said, "Hey Romeo, first Gary, now Bernice, you trying to take all the action?"

Brad added, "Who has it better than Mike?"

John cut in and said, "I stopped them just in time, Bernice probably would've had her teeth out by now."

They collectively responded, "Ewwww!"

Mike busted out laughing, sprayed a few bits of nachos across the bar and gestured slight acceptance.

Kelly added, "Even for me you have a pretty diverse sex life there Mike!"

They all looked at Kelly and she replied, "What?"

Bert came by and asked them what they were drinking.

John replied, "Mikes taking it easy tonight, aren't you Mike, we'll just have a couple of beers."

Mike held up the empty basket of nachos, suggesting Bert should bring some more.

As they were waiting for Bert to return, Al mentioned the disaster at Investco, he added, "That knucklehead Collin is in big trouble, he rewired a circuit board and destroyed a machine, we have to service exchange it now."

They looked at Al in disbelief and Brad replied, "I never thought anyone would be stupid enough to try something like that, you're kidding right?"

Mike started to laugh but stopped and added, "That's just not funny."

Al responded, "Believe it or not the kid's not sorry either, he tried to blame it on their wall power."

John added, "How did Oscar take it, he must be pissed."

Just then, Bert returned with their drinks and Mike's nachos.

Al continued, "Oscar wasn't there."

Mike replied amusingly, "I'll bet he's doing the wild thing with his wild woman," laughed then added, "Now that's funny!"

Kelly replied, "Not if your Lyzette," then thought for a moment and added, "Come to think of it, probably not if your Oscar either."

Mike busted out laughing and replied, "Good one Kelly!"

John added, "You have a one track mind tonight don't you Mike!"

Mike didn't reply but continued eating the nachos.

When he wasn't looking, John emptied the basket and changed the subject.

He asked Al, "Did I hear we have a meeting tomorrow?"

Al replied, "Yeah, Rob is ready to try out the fix for the flaky software, he wants a few of us in his office tomorrow morning, first thing."

Brad added, "Rob is working on some special software for me too, I hope it's ready."

Mike had placed his hand in the empty nacho basket just as Bert came by.

Bert noticed and commented, "Holy crap Mike, you got the munchies? I just filled that thing."

Mike had a puzzled look on his face but replied, "I guess."

He held the basket up and asked for more.

John was right behind Mike and grinning from ear to ear. Bert could tell something was going on but didn't know just what, so he filled the basket again and walked away slightly confused.

Mike still had the munchies and continued eating the nachos.

Al continued, "Oh yeah Mike, Ron was asking about your visual on Tom and Frank the other day, do you remember the exact location?"

Mike waited a second until he swallowed the latest mouthful of nachos and replied, "Absolutely, I was trying to see where in the building they were going just as they were coming out but I can show you the building."

While Mike wasn't looking, John emptied the nacho basket again. This time Brad and Kelly caught on to what he was doing and Kelly told Mike, "What the hell Mike, save some for the rest of us."

Mike looked down in disbelief at the empty basket, noticed Kelly smiling almost uncontrollably and replied, "Kellyyy, what are you smiling about? What's so funny?"

John added, "Yeah Kelly, what did you do?"

Kelly responded, "Me, what about you?"

Then it all unraveled and they had a good laugh. Bert overheard them, came over and noticed the empty basket again. He told Mike, "Jeez, I'm going to start charging you by the pound, why don't you look at the menu for crying out loud!"

John held up a basket that was overflowing with Nachos and Bert added, "I should have known."

They stuck around for a little while longer and had a few laughs but with a meeting scheduled for the morning decided to call it quits early.

The next day started in the office, bright and early. Mike, Brad, Stu, Al and a few other techs gathered in the meeting room. Ron entered and immediately started the meeting.

He explained, "Rob, the regional specialist may have found a fix for the new logic chips and wanted to try it out right away. If you're here, consider yourself a guinea pig."

He added, "After the meeting, go directly to Rob's office and pick up your sets of chips loaded with the latest software. Please guys, we need them installed by tomorrow night at the latest."

Ron dismissed the meeting but asked Mike and Al to return to his office when they were done with Rob.

Along the way to Rob's office, Al, Brad, Stu and Mike talked about the software issue. Mike explained that the problem was driving Bruce nuts at A Force of One, "The guy takes every little thing and turns it into a major catastrophe. He's a real drama queen."

Brad vented his frustration, "Fusia doesn't have time to deal with this crap either,
Jordan's ready to cut my throat over there. We've been on a couple of dates now and it's starting to mess with our relationship, I don't need this."

Al chimed in, "That can't be good, didn't I warn you guys about that!"

They arrived at Rob's office, which was more like a lab. Rob had test equipment set up on a workbench and was in the middle of programming software on another set of logic chips. It was old technology by today's standards but still effective on the older machines.

Brad quickly asked Rob, "Did you finish mine?"

Rob could program the chips to say almost anything he wanted like, "Clear the jam butt hole," or "Help Me!"

Rob showed Brad a set of chips he was just finishing up. He had the front panel from a machine on his test bench that read, "I love you."

Al and Mike looked at each other and started goofing on Brad.

Mike told Brad, "I didn't know you and Rob swung that way, maybe you can hook up with Gary too, I'll take care of Jordan for you."

Brad replied, "Ah c'mon Mike, you'd give up a threesome with Bernice and Gary. Maybe even a foursome if you add Artie."

Mike shuddered and responded, "Ah dude, that's just gross!"

Al looked at Rob and said, "Should we leave you and Brad alone for awhile."

Rob continued and told them he had some that were a little more "R" rated. He held up a set that would display, "Nice rack," and another that read, "Show me your boobs!"

They couldn't help but laugh and high fived Rob.

After they settled down, Al got them back on track. Rob explained he had printed out installation instructions and handed them out.

Mike, Brad and Stu picked out their sets of chips from a pile on Rob's desk.

Rob asked, "So guys, when can I expect to have these installed?"

The guys looked at each other and voiced their plans for the day. They explained to Al that they were tied up and had a full days work planned already.

Al explained, "No matter what, by tomorrow night I promised Ron the chips would be in the machines."

Brad added, "I understand we need to get this done but I hate being a crash test dummy, these tests cause more problems than they fix."

Stu added, "Remember the new clutches, that was a disaster."

Al responded, "I know it can be a pain in the butt, that's why we're only testing them on you guys."

Mike looked at Al and replied, "Thanks Al, what did we ever do to you?" and smiled.

Al looked at the guys and added, "Whatever we need to do, tomorrow night we need them installed, call me today and keep me posted."

After the meeting ended, some of the guy's split up and took calls while Mike and Al headed to Ron's office.

Ron's door was closed when they arrived, Al knocked and Ron called them in. Greg and Collin were seated in front of Ron and they looked very uneasy.

Ron explained to Al, "I wanted you all to hear this together so there's no confusion. Collin, Greg, you are to never alter one of my machines again, ever, in any way, shape or form, do I make myself clear!"

Collin replied, "Why are you so afraid of innovators like me Ron? Where would aviation be today if you were around when the Wright brothers were building their first airplane. We'd all still be riding horses if you were in charge of Henry Ford, what's wrong with you?

Ron added, "Collin, you're right for a change, those are excellent examples of very talented and innovative thinkers. But you forget, as incredible as they are you're just some butt hole who thinks he knows everything about everything. In fact you're an excellent example of someone who knows nothing about anything! Now tell me you'll never alter one of my machines again Collin or go home right now!"

Collin reluctantly replied, "Alright."

Ron turned to Greg and before he could say anything Greg replied enthusiastically, "Absolutely, never, ever!"

Ron continued, "Furthermore, Al is the group specialist and he has my complete confidence, you are never to go against anything he tells you, do you understand!"

Collin and Greg again replied, "Yes."

Ron added, "Good, now go to Renee and see where she needs you, I have to figure out how I'm keep you two from being fired, do you know how much money you two have cost us?"

Collin started to say, "But my Dad.." when Ron cut him off, pointed at the door and added, "Just go Collin, don't say anything, just get out of here!"

As Collin and Greg left, Ron asked Mike and Al to close the door and take a seat. Al commented, "I'm sure Greg had very little to do with destroying that machine."

Mike added, "Please, I've seen Greg's work, he has a more subtle approach to killing machines. He prefers a slower death, drawn out over months of neglect."

Ron replied, "Mike's right, it's still good for Greg to squirm a little, anyway that's not why I called you guy's here. Rob has been working on these bad numbers we've been seeing, he's close to pinpointing a location. Mike, Al tells me you saw Frank and Tom coming out of a building together. It sounds like the same area that Rob suspects is at the heart of our problem. I'm going to need your help pinpointing where Frank and Tom are working, can I count on you both?"

Al looked at Mike and they replied almost in unison, "Of course!"

Ron added, "I knew I could, just keep this between us for now."

Al replied, "I'm afraid it's too late for that, we've already told Brad, John and Kelly."

Ron responded, "Alright but let them know that they are not to tell anyone else, I just know this is going to bite us all in the ass real soon."

Suddenly there was a knock on Ron's door and it opened, it was Chuck who barged in as usual, unannounced.

Ron looked at Al and said, "He's getting better, at least he knocked!"

Mike and Al split up and took calls for the remainder of the morning. At one point during the day, Mike was on the phone with Renee who sounded upset about something but said she couldn't explain.

It was early afternoon when suddenly every tech was texted with a message to come to the office, four pm, no exceptions.

Mike had just arrived at Fusia and was meeting up with Brad who was already onsite. Mike was at the reception desk with Kandi, no one else was there so Kandi was able to talk in her normal voice. Mike was chiding her about the upcoming Yankees, Phillies game when he got the call.

He had never received a call like that before and thought, "This can't be good."

He met up with Brad in the copy center. Brad was sitting at Jordan's desk, talking to Jordan about the text message when he arrived.

Brad told Mike, "This can't be good, they don't call us in like this to give us raises."

Mike added, "Maybe the software issue is bigger than we thought or maybe it had to do with the bogus numbers Ron was concerned about."

Jordan told them both, "Look, I learned a long time ago not to worry about crap like this. It is what it is, your mind will blow it up into something much worse than it probably is."

They admitted she was probably right and finished installing the new chips.

They had to cut it close, it was three forty five and the meeting was due to start at four pm. Brad explained to Jordan he had to go but she could power up and run the machine if needed. He added, "You may be in for a nice surprise," then left.

They arrived at the meeting just as the doors were closing and squeezed their way in.

Chuck stepped up to the podium, tapped on the microphone and asked, "Is this thing on." After not hearing anything, he unplugged a connector and an extremely loud popping noise filled the room. While everyone held their ears, a tech joined Chuck onstage, took care of the problem and the meeting began.

He explained that the main office was cutting back and in an effort to control costs would begin outsourcing the role of dispatch.

Everyone in the room went quiet at first then quickly became very noisy. Most of the dispatchers were seen in tears and everyone around them tried consoling them as best they could.

Chuck continued, "I can't tell you all how deeply upset this makes me, I've come to know you all like family.

This is, however, a plan that came directly from the top and they want to begin testing tomorrow. As calls come in to the dispatch area the system will automatically divert some of them to the overseas dispatch. If successful, dispatch in its entirety will be moved next month."

Mike could see Renee in tears at the front of the auditorium. Al, John and Kelly were doing their best to console her.

Chuck added, "On a lighter note, the end of the quarter is upon us and our district is ahead of everyone in the country. Sales, service revenue, customer satisfaction, all our numbers are up. As a way of saying thank you, the region is having its quarterly meeting here in our district with a party to follow. In light of the dispatch situation, the timing is horrible but you have all worked hard to achieve this recognition, lets try to make the best of it."

He concluded the meeting and Ron told his crew he would buy the first round at Rosie's, dispatchers could drink for free. Mike really wasn't in the mood and felt awful for Renee so he decided to get his software installed.

He called Bruce at A Force of One and Bruce told him, "It's a good thing I know how to push people, see, I get my machine fixed before everyone else, on overtime yet. You know, you should enroll in one of our assertiveness classes Mike, it's good to be force full and get your way. By the way, you know this had better work or else!"

Mike wasn't in the mood for Bruce today so he just blew him off and replied, "Yeah Bruce, you the man," and hung up.

He arrived onsite at A Force of One and it was quiet for a change. Gary and Bruce had gone home already so he could relax. After a couple of hours he finished up, found he was really tired and frustrated, so headed home for the night. He decided he could come back in the morning and test run the machine.

The next morning, Ron and Bill were meeting with Chuck in Ron's office, Chuck was extremely upset. He explained to Ron that the office was about to be over run with corporate people. Vice presidents, techs and management from the entire region would be here for the meeting. If they really scrutinize our numbers carefully their bound to see the screw up. Chuck added, "I'll be ruined, what are you going to do Ron!"

Ron replied, "What am I going to do? What about you, all these screwy numbers started long before I got here, you should have seen this coming a long time ago!"

Chuck responded, "Like I always say.."

Ron cut him off and added, "What do you always say Chuck, never do today what you can put off till tomorrow!"

Bill added, "No, I think it's more like tee off time is at noon!"

Chuck looked up at them both with a scowl and replied, "That's not funny and don't try to lecture me, do you know all I have to do around here, do you think it's easy running this place."

Ron added, "The way you run it, hell yea! When is tee off time today Chuck? It probably is noon, right! You go golfing almost every afternoon, why don't you stay once in awhile and see what goes on around here!"

Chuck replied, "I believe in delegating certain responsibilities to my managers, that is why you're here right? Besides I must be doing something right, I'm receiving an award aren't I?"

Ron responded, "That just tells me that corporate doesn't know what the hell they're doing either. Look Chuck, I have a lead I'm looking into, Mike saw Tom and Frank leaving a building in midtown together and Rob may have narrowed down the location of a suspicious entry on the latest spreadsheet. I'm looking into it and I'll let you know what I find.

Chuck replied, "That's more like it, just keep me in the loop. I have some important things to take care of too you know, when our VP's arrive they'll need to be entertained.

Ron added, "Aren't you forgetting something, you have a dispatch room full of upset dispatchers, don't you think you should be doing something for them? Maybe try to stop this outsourcing crap?"

Chuck replied, "You're right, I'll get right on that. Bill, I'm assigning that too you!"

As Chuck was leaving, Ron overheard him muttering, "Now how soon can I reserve the golf course? I'll get Millie right on that.

Ron then heard Chuck yell, "Millie, drop whatever you're doing, I have a very important job for you.

They heard Millie reply, "So long as I'm done by noon, I have my granddaughter's birthday party this afternoon, you promised I could leave early today!"

Ron asked Bill to close the door as they heard Chuck reply, "You're granddaughter will have plenty of birthdays, this is important. Start calling all the golf courses in the area."

Bill looked at Ron and added, "He wouldn't make her cancel would he?"

Ron replied, "There's nothing he does that surprises me anymore!"

Bill walked towards Ron's window and replied, "It's a shame this window doesn't open, he'd make a great splat down there," and looked out of Ron's window.

As he was looking, Bill saw Ron's building buddy across the street and added, "Holy mother of, look at this girl in the window Ron, across the street!"

Ron looked and replied, "Oh, that's my new friend, hot huh!"

She waved to them and held up her usual sign that read, "Lunch?"

Ron added, "I feel so bad for her, everyday she stands there with that sign asking me to lunch. She almost makes me wish I was single again. Look at the body on that girl, that's got to be the smallest and tightest blue dress I've ever seen."

Ron still didn't realize it but his building buddy was now attracting the attention of at least ten other men and a couple of women from his building.

Bill responded, "Yeah, shame you're married Ron, I just remembered a call I have to make, I'll see you later," then left the room.

As for Mike, He arrived that morning at A Force of One. As he entered the copy room Gary was standing in front of machine. He turned to Mike and it appeared his eyes were welling up with tears. Mike thought, "Oh crap," then asked Gary what was wrong and approached the machine.

Gary threw his arms around Mike and told him, "I knew it Mike, no one can fight true love." Mike tried to break away but Gary was holding him too tight.

Mike looked down at the machine and realized the display panel read, "I love you." Again, Mike tried to break away, he envisioned his Aunt Mary's dog Whitey and the way he tried to break away from him when he was a kid and Whitey was humping his leg.

Mike was able to grab hold of a newspaper from the top of the machine and started smacking Gary in the nose.

Mike told him, "Get off of me you little pervert, this is a mistake."

Gary replied, "True love like ours is never a mistake Mike, stop fighting it."

Mike continued smacking Gary with the newspaper until his grip loosened. Just as Mike got him loose he looked over and realized Bruce had entered the room.

Bruce yelled out, "What are you two doing, stop that immediately, this instant. I don't care what you two do on your own time, but don't do it here."

He looked at Mike and added, "I had no idea Mike."

Mike looked at Bruce and replied, "You have this all wrong, Gary has the wrong idea Bruce."

Bruce looked down at the machine and saw the control panel reading, "I love you." He continued, "I wonder where he could have gotten that idea from."

Mike replied, "Look, Bruce, I put the new software in last night, this is how we found the machine this morning."

Bruce started going off and told Mike, "So the software isn't right, did I not tell you it better work or else."

Mike responded, "Look, let me make some phone calls and figure out what to do."

As Bruce stormed out of the room, Mike looked at Gary and told him, "Down boy, heel," and held the newspaper up. He added, "Why don't you start running some jobs while I make some phone calls."

Gary looked at Mike with a hurt look and said, "You can't fight this forever Mike," and started preparing his jobs for the copier.

Brad had arrived onsite at Fusia early himself but was a little hung over from the get together at Rosie's the night before. It started out in a less than festive mood but after everyone started drinking and talking it loosened up. Everyone hoped the dispatch test would blowup and be a non-event. Titan started overseas dispatching a year ago and their customers hated it. Some of their customers even cancelled their contracts and came over to AYS complaining they were tired of dropped calls and dispatchers who couldn't speak English.

Brad entered the copy room and saw Jordan sitting at her desk, not looking very happy. Brad asked her, "Why the long face?"

She looked at him and replied, "Are you kidding? Nice surprise? I was really starting to like you Brad," as she got up and left the room.

Just then, Brad's phone rang, it was Mike.

Mike explained the weird message on the machine at A Force of One and how Gary was probably making plans for a wedding. Brad laughed then realized Mike had ended up with his chips by mistake. Brad wondered about

Jordan again then looked down at his machines display, it read, "Nice rack!"

Brad told Mike, "That explains Jordan's mood this morning, she's sensitive about her breast size, I don't know why, she's gorgeous."

Jordan had just entered the room and overheard him, she gave him a hug and told him, "I thought you were being a butt hole."

Gary started running his machine and at first it started running like normal until Gary realized the copies were coming out of the top exit instead of the stapling unit as he had selected. Then it started running at high speed and the copies started flying out of the top exit, all over the floor.

Gary gave a shriek and yelled out, "Mike, sweetie, help!"

Mike replied, "Stop calling me that," then turned and noticed what was happening. He told Brad briefly what was going on, then hung up.

Of course Bruce arrived just as Mike was hanging up and yelled at Mike, "What the hell is wrong with this thing. I warned you, look at all my paper! Who's going to pay for all of this?"

Gary was still shrieking and trying to pick up the paper. It was coming out of the machine faster than he could pick it up and he was quickly overwhelmed.

Bruce ran out yelling, "I'm calling Ron, this is nonsense."

Mike tried shutting off the power switch but that didn't work. Eventually, the machine ran out of paper and stopped. He pulled the power plug from the wall, sat on the floor and wondered, "What the hell?"

Brad and Jordan just stared at their machine. After hearing of Mike's dilemma they were reluctant to start making copies.

Jordan told Brad, "You start it,"

Brad replied, "I don't want to start it, you do it,"

Jordan responded, "No you go first."

Brad finally put his fingers to his lips and told Jordan, "Shhhh, here goes."

They watched as the machine started running. Brad turned to Jordan and said, "I guess we got lucky," then Jordan pointed to the machine. Brad turned and saw the paper start flying very rapidly out of the top exit.

Jordan shouted to Brad over the noisy machine, "I just loaded all the paper trays, they're full, what are we going to do."

Brad thought for a moment and told Jordan, "I have an idea, cover me."

Jordan replied, "Be careful."

Brad removed the rear covers and found the master circuit breaker. He told Jordan, "Stand back," as he shut off the breaker. The copier shut off with a loud bang and Brad saw a small plume of smoke come out of the power distribution area followed by the awful smell of burning electronics.

Brad heard Jordan say, "Owwww," just as the machine shut down.

Brad yelled out, "Jordan, are you all right," and rushed over to her.

Jordan showed him a paper cut so Brad kissed her finger and told her, "You know, the machine was supposed to say I love you."

Jordan looked up at Brad and replied, "That's just weird, what the hell am I supposed to do with a copier, that's too kinky for me." She added, "Now if it was you," and stopped.

Brad responded, "I do you know."

Jordan replied, "I do you know what."

Brad told her, "Love you, I love you Jordan."

Jordan gave him a hug, blushed and replied, "I love you too Brad," then after two dates and months of anticipation, finally they kissed.

In the meantime at A Force of One, Mike was on the phone with Al just as Bruce returned to the copy room. Bruce was fuming as usual.

Bruce told Mike, "Hang up that phone right now. Do you have any idea what I've just gone through? I called your dispatch and got someone who spoke no English at all. When I tried to tell him what the hell was going on he didn't understand me. I told him I needed to speak to Ron and he had no idea who I was talking about, no Ron here he said. What's wrong with you people? I need this machine."

Gary let out a shriek and showed Mike a paper cut on his finger from picking up the paper. Mike picked up Gary's arm and shoved the cut finger under Gary's armpit.

He told Bruce, "I'll get a hold of Ron for you and start installing the old software right away." He got back on the phone with Al and told him, "Did you get that?"

Al replied, "Got it, I'll call Ron, just get the machine running again."

After reinstalling the old logic chips, Mike finally got the copier running again. Ron spoke for an hour with

Bruce but it was actually more like a shut up and listen session.

Ron spoke to Mike briefly and told him, "Nice work Romeo, Bruce told me all about you and Gary, didn't Al warn you about office romances," then chuckled.

Mike replied in a somewhat feminine voice, "Now stop that Ronald or I'll give you such a pinch."

He turned, noticed Bruce was standing behind him listening and added, "Damn Bruce, I've got to tie a bell on you or something," then told Ron, " I have to go, I have Bruce here waiting for me."

Ron replied, "You have no luck over there today do you? Just keep me posted," and hung up.

Bruce stared at Mike and after a very uncomfortable pause asked Mike, "So where are we."

Mike replied, "The machine is running now, but we're back to square one with the chips. Run it as best you can for now, do you still want to be the first to get the fix when it's available?"

Bruce actually had nothing to say and just walked away.

Mike thought, "I could get used to that," but knew better.

In the meantime at Fusia, Brad put the old set of chips back into his machine but it wouldn't power up. It seems the plume of smoke he saw was something shorting out. Brad had called Al earlier but he was tied up on another problem with Greg and Collin. Something about a chain they replaced on a paper feeder that now does not work. Mike called Brad and found out what was going on. He recalled Al telling him about Stu and what a great tech he actually was. Stu was usually unreachable by phone so Mike asked Brad if there was anywhere he hung out.

Brad explained to Mike, "He has his parts in the basement of his financial account, you might find him on the top shelf of his parts rack, he made a bed up there." Mike told Brad he would stop there first then meet him at Fusia.

Mike had never been to the account before and didn't realize the building had three levels underground. The guard knew Stu very well and explained to Mike just how to find his parts area.

When Mike arrived it wasn't hard to find Stu, as soon as he opened the door you could hear him snoring. Mike climbed to the top of the parts rack and found Stu, just as Brad had described. Stu had made a bed with bubble wrap and some foam from various parts he received, he was all curled up and comfy but drooling from the corner of his mouth. Mike thought, "Gross," and gently gave Stu a shove.

Stu responded, "But Mom, I don't wanna go to school today," and rolled over. Mike gave a chuckle then grabbed some of the bubble wrap and gave it a twist then yelled, "Stu!" The bubble wrap gave a bunch of loud pops and Stu shot up with his arms flailing wildly. Stu looked at his watch and said, "It's not time to go home yet, what am I doing up."

He rolled over to go back to sleep and suddenly noticed Mike there. At first he stared in disbelief then asked Mike, "What the hell are you doing here?"

Mike explained to Stu all that was going on and that they needed his help. Stu listened as Mike described what Brad's machine was doing.

Stu explained in detail just what an abrupt power down would do and told Mike to go to the parts depot, pickup two circuit boards and the relay from the power control unit then added, "Mike, I promise that will fix it, now let me get back to sleep."

After battling his way through the crowds, he picked up two of the parts from the parts depot but the relay was out of stock. He had Renee run a check and found that another tech on the west side said he had one. After another half hour of battling crowds he arrived at an office building and was escorted by a security guard to a mailroom. Once there he was greeted by a machine operator who asked Mike, "Please tell me you're here to fix my machine!"

Mike replied, "Sorry, I'm just here to pick up a part from another tech, is Dave here?"

The operator responded, "Come on, I'll take you to the machine," and added, "I'm never going to get my copy job done."

As Mike approached the machine he saw it was in pieces and recognized two techs sitting at a table playing cards, it was two of the smucks from the park.

They saw Mike and told him to wait a minute till they finished playing their hand. One of them got excited and yelled, "Fish!"

They then got up, greeted Mike and introduced themselves as Daryl and Darla. Mike thanked them for the part and started to introduce himself when suddenly the mailroom manager appeared and was extremely angry.

He yelled at Daryl, "Are you finally done with your lunch, is there anything else I can get you. Maybe an espresso or a latté, you guys are killing me here. I have three jobs that have to be done today. Fix this freaking machine already!"

Daryl replied, "No need to get nasty, were working as fast as we can here, let me wake up Dave," and walked behind the machine.

The mailroom manager followed Daryl to the back of the machine. Dave had a cot setup behind it and frequently napped behind his machine.

The manager yelled, "Dave! Get the hell up and fix my machine, or perhaps you need a little wake up snack or shower or martini. It's always something with you guy's.

Dave responded, "Jeez buddy, you better switch to decaf or something, you're a little high strung. I don't appreciate the attitude either, how'd you like to wake up to that?"

The manager was fuming by now and replied, "If this machine's not running in an hour I'm throwing it out of the window along with you and your two other morons!"

Dave replied, "We'll have you up and running right away!"

Dave looked at Mike and added, "Don't mind him, he's just a little high strung. You're here for the relay, right?"

Mike replied, "I'd appreciate it, I have a machine down too and my team mate is desperate."

Dave replied, "No problem and reached down into the machine, removed the relay and handed it to Mike."

Mike and Dave saw Daryl heading over to the window with a measuring tape, Dave asked Daryl, "What are you doing?"

Daryl replied, "Didn't you hear him, I'm checking the window. I don't think the machines going to fit."

Dave responded, "He's right, you're a moron!"

Dave then looked at Mike and added, "I have to think of everything with these two."

Dave looked at Daryl and added, "You have to measure the machine with the covers off."

Dave looked at Mike again and said, "See what I have to deal with."

Mike shook his head in disbelief and thanked him for the part then wished him luck with his customer.

On the way out he turned back and noticed Darla working on the machine. She turned and noticed Mike looking her way so she smiled and waved at him. Mike didn't realize it earlier but she was actually an attractive girl, in her low twenties with long red hair she wore in a ponytail. Mike waved back and thought, "How did she ever hook up with those two?"

It took a while but Mike finally arrived at Fusia with the parts. Kandi had clients in the reception area so she greeted Mike with her snooty attitude and Australian accent but gave him a wink when they weren't looking.

As Mike arrived at the copy room, Brad was helping Jordan with her work.

Jordan told Mike, "I am so behind in my work, I hope you have good news."

Brad added, "Did you find Stu?"

Mike replied, "Yes and Yes, Stu thinks he knows what's wrong and swears these will fix it. You won't believe what I went through to get these parts though."

He described the situation he encountered with the smucks. Brad wasn't surprised at all but Jordan replied, "For getting me out of this jam I'll be the first to say thank you, they do sound like people of rare intelligence though.

Brad replied, "Yeah, rare that they use any!"

Mike added, "Come on, let's be glad they gave us the part, I know I owe them one. Then added, "By the way Jordan, where the hell is my latté."

She laughed, balled up a piece of paper and threw it at him then added, "Smart ass!"

After an hour of installing the parts, they looked at each other, connected the power cord and reluctantly hit the power switch.

Mike stayed behind the machine to watch for smoke and as it started powering up he gave a blood-curdling scream. Brad and Jordan could see Mike's legs flailing wildly and shut the machine off. They immediately ran to the back yelling, "Mike are you alright!"

When they got to the back of the machine they saw him laying there with a huge grin. Mike added, "Made you look!"

Jordan gave him a couple of smacks and told him, "What's wrong with you, don't kid around like that, you scared the crap out of me."

Brad told him, "You know we will get even with you for that."

They powered up again, this time Brad watched for smoke and all went well. The copier finally came back to life and Jordan put a job on it as soon as it was ready.

It was getting close to five o'clock and they figured Stu might pick up his phone if they called him. Stu actually answered and agreed to meet them at Rosie's. They contacted Al and John who said they would meet them there as well. Mike and Brad waited for Jordan to finish her work and headed to Rosie's.

When they arrived it was semi busy but they found room at the bar. Bert got to them and asked Jordan, "Is everything alright miss? You're not high on crack or anything are you?"

Jordan looked at Bert with a surprised look and replied, "Excuse me? Why would you think something like that?"

Bert responded, "When I see someone as beautiful as you sitting here with these two I know your standards must be pretty low or something has to be wrong."

They laughed and Bert brought over their first round just as Stu was coming in.

They were surprised to see Stu with a very attractive young woman he introduced as Carol and apparently was one of his operators.

They welcomed Stu and his friend then bought them a round.

Stu asked, "So how did you make out with your machine Brad?"

Brad replied, "You're fix worked like a charm." They thanked Stu and Jordan gave him a hug for figuring out what was wrong with her copier.

Mike asked Stu, "So, now that we have you awake, tell me, how did your set of chips workout."

Stu looked at Carol and asked, "Should we tell them?"

Carol gave the cutest, almost juvenile laugh, then said, "Um, ok," then started raising her blouse.

Mike and Stu, who were closest to Carol stopped her and Stu added, "No, I said should we tell them, not show them."

Carol chuckled again and said, "Oh."

Stu explained, "You know, Rob may be a brain and all but he screws up a lot. He gave me the wrong chips too, mine said show me your boobs."

Carol said, "Ok," and started to raise her blouse again, Mike stopped her and added, "You could poke an eye out with those things!"

Carol gave another cute laugh, looked at Mike and said, "You're funny."

Brad cut in and said, "Mike is spoken for Carol," and started telling them about Mikes experience with Gary at A Force of one.

Carol added, "That's a shame Mike, you're cute."

Mike laughed and told them, "Thanks, now she thinks I'm gay, and now that I think about it, how fair is this. Brad, you end up with a fox like Jordan. Stu, you end up with this gorgeous lady and I end up with Gary throwing himself all over me, it's not fair."

Brad added, "Let's not forget about Bernice."

Stu replied, "Bernice? Dude, you really have to raise your standards!"

Al and John were just coming in and overheard Mike's comment.

John added, "Mike's gay? I can attest to that."

Carol added, "You're gay too?"

By now the whole side of the bar was caught up in the conversation and was having a great laugh.

Mike brought up his experience with the west side techs and added, "Whoever nicknamed them smucks was right."

Suddenly it dawned on Mike that Dave removed the relay from the machine that had to be up and running rather than from his parts locker.

Mike mentioned this to his team mates and they all burst into laughter.

John responded, "It wouldn't surprise me, I can see them trying to figure out why their machine isn't powering up right now, smucks!"

Brad added, "How do people like that keep their jobs?"

Al explained that at least one of them must have family in high places or they could never get away with the crap they pull.

John added, "Not like our buddy Stu here I guess."

Stu replied, "Hey, I have nothing to prove, I never wanted this job anyway. My parents forced me into this, I really want to open one of those mattress stores but on a large scale, you know like a depot."

They all laughed and Al replied, "You know Stu, that would suit you!"

John stretched his arms and let out a yawn, Mike noticed and asked John if he had a late night. Brad overheard and replied, "Don't get him started!"

John became agitated and explained that his Grandmother came home from Bingo with some old fart she picked up. John added, "The old bird is a screamer and had me up all freaking night! You don't want to know about all the other noises that old people make. If I ever get my hands on the butt hole who invented Viagra I'm going to strangle them!"

Everyone at the bar replied almost in unison, "Ewwwww!"

Brad added, "You know, if you reach a point where it doesn't work anymore you should let it be!

John added, "Amen to that!"

The conversation eventually turned to the dispatch problem and Al explained, "You know, our friend Bruce may have actually helped us for a change. After Ron got an earful from Bruce, he had him talk to Chuck. Chuck had one of the VPs with him so he had Bruce give him an earful too. As if that wasn't enough, the VP's whole morning was shot listening to customers like Bruce and they were all pissed off. I'm hearing that calls were being dropped all day, customers were waiting for hours with no one calling them back and no one could understand a word the dispatchers were saying!"

John added, "It probably won't change anything, all these big shots care about is the bottom line."

Al replied, "We'll see."

Brad then asked Al about his day with Collin and Greg.

Al responded, "That knucklehead is driving me nuts. You know what he did? He tried to rebuild the paper feeder and put the chain on backwards. Then I tried to explain what he did and he wouldn't hear it, he tried to blame it on Greg but Greg was perfectly clean as usual. In the mean time Collins hands were black with chain grease. I'm telling you I can't take him anymore, at least acknowledge when you screw up and learn from it."

Just then, Mike's phone rang, it was a number he wasn't familiar with and thought, "I'll probably regret this," but answered the call anyway. It was Daryl, one of the smucks who had given him the part earlier.

Mike could hear someone yelling in the background and Daryl asked, "Do you still have that relay, Dave needs it back!"

Mike replied, "Just a minute, let me see if I can get it back." Mike then asked Brad and Jordan, "Our friend needs the relay back, can we get back into Fusia."

Jordan responded, "They're closed, no one is allowed back in there after six o'clock, tell him I'm really sorry."

Mike explained to Daryl that it was too late and Al yelled into the phone that he could still order the part for overnight delivery. Mike added, "I feel for you Daryl but it's too late."

As he hung up, Al could tell that Mike felt bad for the smucks and added, "Don't feel bad Mike, that crew is so stupid I heard they passed the YMCA and thought the Macy's sign was spelled wrong."

Everyone laughed and Stu cut in, "Dave is so dumb he thinks cheerios are donut seeds."

Brad added, "Those three were the inspiration for that saying, a mind is a terrible thing to waste."

Mike cut in, "Alright already, I get it, I still feel bad for the guy though."

Al replied, "It doesn't pay to be stupid Mike but don't worry, they've been pulling stuff like that long before you got here. I'm sure they're going to be just fine."

They realized it was getting late so decided to call it a night.

Al pulled Mike, Brad and John aside and explained that they were to meet in Ron's office in the morning, he had a special job for them.

Back on City Island, Angela had just finished putting Katie to bed. Her and Ron were sitting in their backyard, watching the sun go down. It was a warm beautiful night on the bay and they were snuggling on the chase lounge. Ron decided it would be a good time to bring up the news of his building buddy.

Ron described how this woman kept appearing in the window across from his, in the building across the street and asking about lunch. He continued, "I kind of feel bad for the girl, I keep telling her no but she's persistent. I don't know if she's having a problem with her job or what, I'd hate for something to happen to her."

Angela replied, "You're so sweet, worried about that poor girl, how old did you say she is?"

Ron responded, "I couldn't tell, it's so far away."

Angela added, "You know, Katie's gym teacher keeps telling me that he teaches aerobics up in New Rochelle, not far from here. You should see him Ron, he has the most muscular, chiseled physique. He keeps asking me to join his classes, you think I should?"

Angela knew Ron was extremely jealous and would never allow it. However, she could tell Ron was feeling her out, if she gave her permission he would be having lunch with the tart in no time. By telling him about the gym teacher she'd stop him dead in his tracks. Still, she felt good that Ron would at least talk to her about it so figured a reward, no, more like a reminder was in order. Make sure he remembered what he had at home.

Angela reached down and rubbed Ron's leg gently in just the spot she knew would get his attention and said, "You know, all this talk is getting me excited, how about you?"

Ron replied, "You're reading my mind honey, do you still have that blue dress? No wait a minute, the red one!"

Chapter 8 - The End – Almost

Ron arrived at his office extra early this morning and was as prepared as he could be for a very stressful day. Chuck was driving him crazy as usual and was trying to delegate anything and everything that required thought or action. With Bill volunteered to handle the possible outsourcing issue and dispatch, Ron still had the parts and rogue IP address issue to deal with. Add to that the logic and software problem that was hanging over his head plus Collin and Greg were becoming a bigger problem than even he anticipated.

He looked out of his window and thought, "I'm starting to hate this job again!"

Of course Chuck's only concern was entertaining the big shots from the home office while they are in town. Even if it meant forcing Millie to cancel her plans for her granddaughter's birthday party. Chuck was determined to keep all of these issues from them, giving the appearance that he was always in control of a tightly run district.

Ron thought to himself, "You can only sweep stuff under the carpet for so long before someone notices a pile of crap."

He had just sat down when there was a knock at the door, it was Al, Mike and Brad. Ron commented, "Oh no, are you guy's ganging up on me already."

Al replied, "I guess you heard about our day yesterday?"

Ron responded, "Mostly from Mike, did you and Gary set a date yet Mike?"

Mike replied, "Funny, I'm starting to think I should get hazardous duty pay over there, it's getting harder and harder to keep away from him.

Brad added, "Please Mike, you're getting all the action lately, first Gary, now Bernice, who's next?"

Ron replied, "Mike, we have to do something about you, get you back on track. Al, can't we take up a collection, hook Mike up with Gil's friends at the strip club?"

Then, another knock on the door, this time it was Rob with the latest data from the parts issue. He entered and Mike was the first to greet him.

Mike smiled and commented, "Rob, am I ever glad to see you, do you know what your software is doing to me? My operator Gary at A Force of One got the chips you set up for Brad, Gary thinks we're in love now, I literally can't turn my back on the guy anymore!"

Rob replied, "Oh c'mon Mike, I've been to A Force of one, you and Gary would make a cute couple," and chuckled.

Ron added, "Al, don't we have a tool number for a butt plate we can order Mike?"

Mike replied with a smile, "Let's just say I owe you one Rob."

Then Brad added, "The chips I got put me in hot water with my girl at Fusia."

Rob replied, "Almost? Did it work out?"

Brad responded, "Yeah but it was close."

Rob replied, "Then there you go, what's the problem?"

Al added, "Haven't I been warning you guy's about office romances."

Ron replied, "Especially you Mike, two in two days, you hound!"

Ron then added, "Seriously though Rob, what happens next with the software?"

Rob added, "Well, it's back to the drawing board. In case you haven't heard, all software is experimental. When they come out with a new version, whether it's an operating system, game or I don't care what, it's usually to correct flaws in the original software. Unfortunately the new software usually comes with its own new bugs so it's always back to the drawing board. You've heard of plug and play, it's really plug and pray."

Al asked, "When can we expect the next fix?"

Rob replied, "I can only keep you posted."

Ron then changed the subject to the parts issue and asked Rob, "Have you pinpointed the location of our rogue IP address?"

Rob then laid out a map of the city on Ron's desk, he had circled a specific city block in the midtown area.

Rob added, "This is the source of our bogus numbers, I'm sure of it."

Mike pointed out it was where he saw Tom and Frank so they agreed to head there later in the morning and observe what they could.

Rob added, "I looked into your suggestion Ron, because we pay the bill for Franks phone we can legally track his location using his phones serial number. I've already used it and marked on the map where he's been hanging his hat the last few days.

Ron replied, "That's great, we can use that info in so many ways, can you track him throughout the day and keep us posted?"

Rob replied, "I'd like to but Bill already has me working on the overseas dispatch problem."

Ron responded, "That's important too, can you take one of my guys and set them up to monitor Frank?"

Rob replied, "Sure thing, it's not difficult once I establish the connection, all they have to do is monitor a blip on a screen."

Ron looked at Brad and asked, "What do you think Brad, you up for it."

Brad responded, "You know I am!"

Ron replied, "That's what I need to hear! Then added, "Al, Mike, why don't you guys make plans to head to the building where Mike last saw Frank and Tom. I'm sure you won't see them until late morning so talk to Renee and help clean up any open calls, then head to the location. Make sure you keep in touch with Brad, I'll make sure John and Kelly are available if you need them.

Just then, Al received a call from Renee. Collin and Greg were at Sloppy Copy and getting into trouble already.

Al rolled his eyes and asked Ron, "Can I shoot them Ron, please. You can tell the judge I went off, they pushed me over the edge, please, can I?"

Ron replied, "Let me guess, Collin? Then smiled and added, "The line forms behind me Al, besides, I have a plan, there's a reason why Collin hasn't been traveling with you."

Al responded, "I just thought you were being nice to me."

Ron replied, "I am, but if this kids going to sink himself I don't want you to be overly involved, just enough to be able to say you bailed him out once in awhile, just trust me."

They finished up the meeting and Al headed to Sloppy Copy, it wasn't busy so Mike joined Al and hoped they could finish up early.

They arrived onsite and Mike entered first as Al stopped outside to tie his shoe. Gil saw Mike and remarked, "Oh no, they must be desperate, they sent you?"

Mike replied, "Watch it; I'll get Kelly after you."

Gil responded, "I'd pay extra for that."

Apparently Gil had taken a liking to Kelly ever since that night in the ring.

Al walked through the door and Gil remarked, "I feel better now, I thought you were sticking me with Mike," and smiled. He added, "I'd take Mike any day over those two you sent over."

Mike responded, "That's not saying much Gil."

Al asked, "So what are the little knuckleheads up to?"

Gil replied, "Besides driving us all crazy, come see for yourself."

Gil brought them over to the machine, Collin and Greg were arguing over something. Al realized that Collin was trying to alter the cleaning system and Greg was trying his best to stop him.

Al asked Collin, "So what's the problem?"

Collin replied, "This cleaning system can't work right the way it's set up. You're choking the vacuum."

Al responded, "What was the problem with the machine when you started?"

Greg replied, "They were getting dirty copies."

Al asked Collin, "What have you checked so far?"

Collin replied, "Nothing, I'm telling you the vacuum is too low, it needs to be rerouted. If we increase the vacuum you'll never have that problem again."

Al remembered what Ron had mentioned earlier about Collin sinking himself and responded, "Alright Collin, give it a shot, lets see what you've got."

Mike looked at Al and wondered what he was up to; Collin had already destroyed enough equipment.

Mike asked Al, "Should I call 911?"

Collin started removing hoses and rerouted them in a strange configuration Al had never seen before. After a few minutes Collin finished and announced, "I just improved the efficiency by thirty percent."

Al replied, "What about the mess, don't you need to clean it up."

Collin responded, "I just did my part, there are four of us here, let someone else do something. What about Mike, can't he get dirty?"

Al replied, "Mike's never been afraid to get dirty, besides, this is your call. Either you, Greg or both of you need to fix this thing."

Greg picked up the hose and reluctantly started cleaning the machine. At one point he started to complain to Al, "You know Mike is the rookie here, I'm the senior, aren't you going to back me up?"

Al pointed and replied, "I think you missed a spot over there Greg."

Collin commented, "You know he's right, Mike is still a rookie."

Mike replied, "At least I finished training douche bag!"

Gil responded, "This is getting good, should I call the gym and reserve the ring for you guys?"

Al told everyone, "Get to work and finish up already."

Greg continued and finally finished cleaning the machine. They powered up the copier and realized they were missing vacuum somewhere. Collin removed a hose and told Greg to turn the vacuum on. As the vacuum energized, a thick stream of black toner poured out of the hose, engulfing Greg and Collin. They were pinned against the wall and couldn't see anything; it was a full scale toner blowout!

Al could see Collin reach for the circuit breaker on the machine and tried to tell him to stop. Collin ignored him and triggered the circuit breaker which created a spark. With the fine powder engulfing the area behind the machine, the spark ignited the powder and suddenly a loud explosion rocked the area followed by a flash fire.

Gil quickly ran to the main circuit breaker on the other side of the room and removed power to the machine. The flash fire quickly put itself out but it was too late for Collin and Greg, they were covered from head to toe in black toner. Because of the intense heat the toner dried like a sheet of plastic or crust. As they slowly stepped away from the wall, Mike and Al saw a perfect silhouette of where they were pinned.

At first, Al and Mike were concerned for Collin and Greg but quickly realized they were alright. They tried their best to hold back but couldn't and busted out laughing.

Gil came over with a camera, as Greg started opening his eye's Gil told him, "Smile assholes!"

Mike added, "You know, that color suits you Greg." Mike saw this as payback for all the work Greg had left him in his old territory.

Al commented, "So Collin, what have we learned, are you ready to stop screwing around with the equipment?"

Collin said nothing as he and Greg quietly headed to the bathroom to cleanup.

Gil asked Al, "What about my machine guy's, I still need it fixed."

Al looked at Mike and responded, "Feel like getting dirty?"

It took a couple of hours but they finally set the vacuum hoses back to normal and cleaned the machine as best they could. They made a list of parts to order but eventually realized the machine would never run right again. Collin had killed another machine and Ron was going to be pissed.

Mike found a piece of paper stuck in the cleaning unit, which was the source of the original problem. Collin wouldn't hear it and claimed Al had planted it there to make him look bad. Either way, Collin and Greg were both overwhelmed and were going to go home early but Ron asked that Collin report to his office immediately. Al figured it would probably take Collin and Greg a couple of days to really clean themselves up. Mike could swear Collin was missing his eyebrows but he was too dirty to be sure.

Al decided to leave the wall behind the machine dirty; it would be a fitting reminder of the day Greg got dirty. Mike couldn't believe it, the wall had a perfect silhouette of Greg and Collin imprinted on it, a perfect monument.

After finishing up at Sloppy copy they got the word from Brad to start heading to midtown. Brad was monitoring Frank and he was on the move, Ron had requested that Collin meet him in his office ASAP.

Back at the office, Bill was in Ron's office, venting about his own problems.

Bill added, "I don't suppose you have room for a few more screwballs on your team?"

Ron replied, "You're kidding right, Al already filled me in about those three. You know most of the other teams in the city have nicknamed them the smucks, right. I'm hearing if stupidity ever becomes a profession those three are set for life!"

Bill responded, "Around here being stupid can make you a district manager in no time. I wish I could argue with that nickname but it fits, they just don't think! How do you give away a part you're going to need to get your machine running? Now I have an angry customer on my hands. If they don't get that part today I'm screwed!"

Ron added, "I just heard that Collin and Greg destroyed another machine; let me know if you need the part, you can always scavenge the part from Sloppy Copy."

Ron changed the subject to the outsourcing project.

Bill told Ron, "I'm at my wits end with that too! I showed the home office in black and white that this plan makes no sense. The customers hate it, all day yesterday it was one dropped call after another. We recorded the calls that made it through and we could hardly understand the dispatchers. Three customers have already threatened to cancel their contracts. We still don't know why but we're already losing customers on the east side, we don't need this!"

Ron replied, "I walk through dispatch and it's like a funeral parlor, Renee seems like she had the life sucked out of her. I don't know how but we have to stop this!"

Bill responded, "We added up all the costs and the home office is right in one respect, they will save some money moving dispatch overseas, for now. Once they start losing customers over crappy service it'll be a whole different story."

Ron replied, "Yeah but don't forget, most of these VP's will just blame it all on us. They'll say we failed to follow through or some other crap, they take credit for everything and responsibility for nothing."

Bill responded, "At best it will mess with one of their afternoon golf outings, for one day anyway. Then they'll look for something else they can dismantle or cut instead of buildup."

Ron noticed that Bill was staying close to his window and looking out frequently. Ron asked Bill, "Are you looking for something out there, making any new friends or maybe a buddy?"

Bill laughed and replied, "As a matter of fact, I'm worried about my guy's. We have an install going on today and the machine has to be wheeled through a parking lot. Kind of looks like rain don't you think?"

Ron looked out of the window and noticed it was mostly sunny in the city with one large cloud off in the distance, still in New Jersey. He replied sarcastically, "Looks like we better call the National weather service Bill, that's a real storm heading our way."

Ron looked across the street and saw his building buddy waving to him from the building next door.

Ron returned the wave and added, "Hey Bill, look at this, my buddy is back."

Bill immediately rushed to the window and they could see she was wearing this really short metallic looking outfit.

Bill responded, "You know I almost forgot, I have an important phone call to make and rushed out of Ron's office."

Ron laughed and thought to himself, "I'll bet you do."

He looked again as his building buddy bent over, revealing just how short her dress actually was.

Ron thought out loud, "Oh man, I've got to call Angie, right away!"

He picked up his phone and was starting to call Angie when suddenly there was a knock on his door, it was Collin.

Ron responded, "Crap!"

Collin took a seat in front of Ron and Ron did all he could to not bust out laughing. Collin looked almost comical, he was missing one eyebrow and his clothes were dirty and singed in a few areas. The fused and dried toner formed plastic like lines on his clothing everywhere there was a wrinkle.

Ron commented, "You making a fashion statement there Collin."

Collin replied, "Excuse me, are you trying to be funny?"

Ron replied, "For now, you're lucky I'm in a good mood, do you know how much damage you've caused over at Sloppy Copy. Not only do we have to replace their machine but Gil is making up an estimate for the insurance company. This is going to cost us big Collin!"

Ron composed himself and added, "Didn't I warn you about redesigning the equipment, you refuse to learn Collin, now we have to pay big money for it!"

Collin replied, "You keep insisting I don't know what I'm doing, I'm tired of it! Why are you all so jealous of me?"

Ron responded, "No one is jealous of you Collin, you have no idea what you're doing. You were thrown out of training, thrown out of Investco, you've destroyed multiple machines and at least two more had to be put back together by someone else. Admit it Collin, this is not your line of work!"

Colin replied, "I'm glad you finally admit it, I belong in engineering or management."

Ron responded, "In therapy is more like it!"

Collin responded, "This is your last chance Ron, I'm calling my dad when I leave here, his friend will call you and by tomorrow I'll be sitting in your chair!"

Ron replied, "I'm done wasting my time with you Collin. You're a spoiled, arrogant and delusional little boy. Get out of my office and don't come back, tell your daddy I said so!"

Collin didn't say a word and judging by the shade of red on his face, Ron could tell he was very angry. Collin left and Ron muttered under his breath, "Who's your daddy now!"

While the door was open, Chuck barged in and started whining about not being able to schedule the golf course for twenty people.

Ron responded, "How about two teams of ten?"

Chuck replied, "That might work," then left the room.

Ron rolled his eyes, formed his hand into a gun, held his finger to his head and pulled the imaginary trigger.

Over in Midtown, Mike and Al arrived at the building where Frank had been seen. The building had entrances on forty second and forty third streets so they had to split up to cover both.

Mike bought a newspaper and positioned himself at the entrance on forty second street. Al put on an old pullover hat he had stuffed in his pocket and waited at the forty third street entrance.

Brad advised them that Frank was only a few blocks away so they waited.

After a couple of hours had gone by they were both getting tired of standing around. Mike bent over to stretch and as he came up he turned and recognized Tom passing right next to him. Mike let him pass and followed him into the building, calling Al along the way. Luckily Tom did not seem to recognize him so Mike was able to follow a short distance behind and watched as Tom entered a stairwell. After Tom let the stairwell door close behind him, Mike looked through a small window and watched Tom enter a room just off of the stairwell.

Mike gently tried turning the doorknob but realized it was locked. He put his ear to the door and overheard Tom talking to someone. He backed away and took a position in the stairwell a half flight up. He was still hidden from view but could see all that was going on below him. Mike then contacted Al and was told that Frank was on the move and heading their way. Al decided to wait and be sure that Frank was heading to the same location.

It wasn't long before Frank arrived and joined Tom in the room just below Mike. Al had followed Frank and now joined Mike in the stairwell. Together they called Brad and advised him, "Tell Ron his geese have landed, goose poopy one and two are in view."

Brad replied, "I'll alert the troops."

Mike and Al waited for at least a half hour until they saw Frank and Tom open the door then leave the room. Mike overheard Frank say they were heading to the lunch cart.

After they left, Mike and Al went downstairs and tried the doorknob, it was unlocked!

They slowly opened the door, peered inside and saw row after row of parts, stacked at least four feet high and marked, "At Your Service Copiers."

Al stared in amazement and told Mike, "Holy crap, do you have any idea how much money is in this room, this is a small fortune in parts!"

They saw no one else around but suddenly heard Toms voice coming up behind them. They moved quickly into the room and hid behind a row of parts boxes.

Tom entered first followed by Frank who commented, "I might need your help later, that machine is kicking my ass man!"

Tom replied, "Come on Frank, can't you fix anything on your own?"

Frank responded, "We're getting too busy lately, this used to be fun. Are we gonna get some help soon?"

Tom replied, "Talk to the boss not me!"

Then Al and Mike heard a voice that sounded familiar to Al, he looked at Mike and motioned that he was going to try and look. Al slowly lifted his head and realized he was just behind Frank then dropped back down without being seen. Unfortunately he could not see who the familiar voice belonged to.

They listened as the third voice explained, "Were on target to have a great year, we'll start looking for help soon. It's not easy to recruit though, this isn't exactly legal you know."

They could then hear who ever it was that was speaking walk away followed by a door closing. Al then heard another set of footsteps followed by a voice that said, "Yo, what the hell are you doing here?"

It was Tom and he was looking right at them.

Al and Mike slowly stood up and Al replied, "Tom, I'm impressed, this looks like quite an operation you have going on here. I'm so glad you landed on your feet."

Al then looked at his watch and added, "Look at the time, we really have to get going, you know how Renee can be."

Tom stopped him and replied, "You never did know when to shut up, shut the hell up already!"

Tom then looked at Mike and said, "I remember you, you were in the office when Ron cut me loose, you took my place you little bastard, I owe you one!"

Frank added, "Now what do we do, you said we'd never get caught."

Tom replied, "First thing I'm going to do is throw a beating on them, I've been waiting for this!"

Tom moved towards Mike but Mike quickly moved out of his way and threw a large box in front of Tom. Tom tripped over the box and fell to the floor. Tom quickly got up but Mike was already two rows of parts away.

While this was going on, Al also was able to move away from Frank.

Tom was angry and suddenly threw himself through the first row of parts that Mike was using for cover. As Tom headed straight for Mike he told Frank, "Get hold of Al and don't let him get away.

Frank told Al, "Stay there and don't make me hurt you," then headed for Al.

Al replied, "Yeah Frank, I'm going to stand still and wait for you, that'll happen!"

Tom was just a few feet away from Mike when Mike side stepped him and got away again. Mike grabbed a part and was getting ready to hit Tom over the head with it when suddenly the front door opened.

Al looked at the man at the door and said, "Sam, what are you doing here?"

Mike realized it was the parts delivery driver who had caused him so much grief. Without hesitation, Mike threw the part at Sam, just missing his head.

Sam responded, "You freaking tool, let me show you how it's done!"

Suddenly a free for all broke out and parts started flying everywhere.

Sam threw a part at Mike just as Tom was lunging for him. The part missed Mike and struck Tom instead. Frank had got his hands on Al and Mike was just about to be cornered by Sam and Tom.

Suddenly there was another voice at the door; it was Ron, standing there along with Brad, John, Kelly and Chuck.

Ron shouted, "Everyone, knock it off!"

They all turned and looked at one another, in silence at first until Chuck spoke. He looked at Sam and asked, "What's going on here, where did all these parts come from Sam?"

Sam replied, "It's this new kid Mike and your new patsy Ron over there. They said my son would be fired if I didn't bring all these parts over here."

Chuck looked at Mike and responded, "Mike, how could you?"

Ron rolled his eyes, looked at Chuck and replied, "Chuck, how long has this been going on? How long have Mike and I been working here?

Chuck looked puzzled so Al responded, "It couldn't be them Chuck, do the math!"

As Chuck started counting on his fingers a part came flying across the room just missing Ron. It came from Tom who remarked, "Your ass is mine, I owe you big!"

Without another word Tom started charging at Ron. He resembled a bull as he plowed through a row of boxes and continued towards Ron. Ron didn't move but stood there waiting until Tom was just inches away."

Even Kelly was getting nervous and commented, "Ron, do you have a death wish, do something!"

Just as Tom lunged for him, Ron stepped to his left, pulled his hands from behind him revealing a heavy rubber drive roller he had picked up off of the floor earlier. Ron smacked Tom on his head and Tom crashed into a pile of boxes. Tom laid there, in pain and added, "Oh crap, my back, can someone help me up?"

Ron replied, "You're kidding right!"

Suddenly, in the confusion, Sam started running for the door. John chased after him until Mike yelled out, "Hold it John, I've got this one!"

Mike picked up a small rectangular box with just the right weight and threw it at Sam. The trajectory couldn't have been better; it arched perfectly and hit Sam in the back of his knees.

Sam hit the floor and laid there as John ran over to make sure he didn't try to get away again.

Mike added, "Strrriike!"

Just then the Police arrived and Ron explained to them all that had happened.

Al pulled Ron and Chuck aside and explained, "There's at least one more person here, his voice is familiar but I'm not sure who he is," and pointed down a hallway.

Together they made their way down the narrow hallway until they reached a door and heard a voice on the other side.

Ron knocked and the man's voice responded, "Come in."

Chuck looked at Al and said, "It can't be!"

Ron opened the door and stepped in, followed by Chuck and Al.

Al remarked, "You're behind this, why!"

Chuck added, "How could you do this to me, after all I've done for you!"

It was Al's former manager, Jack.

Jack replied, "You're kidding, right, I hate you Chuck! You are the most insensitive, uncaring, laziest and most indecisive excuse for a boss I've ever worked for. All you ever care about is yourself and your precious afternoon golf outings. You left me hanging out to dry one too many times; you never supported me when I tried to get a handle on your stupid team of screwballs. So don't ask me how I could do this to you, you made it too easy!"

Chuck looked at Ron to come to his defense but Ron looked at Chuck and replied, "Don't look at me, it's not like I haven't told you that myself!"

Jack looked at Ron and asked, "I don't believe we've met, you are?"

Ron replied, "I'm Ron, I guess I'm your replacement."

Jack responded, "You have my sympathy's Ron."

Ron replied, "You know full well I need them Jack, you certainly have mine."

The police entered the office and started getting statements from everyone.

Al sat at Jack's computer and stared at the open screen. It was very similar to the parts screen they used at their office

Al called Rob and advised him of the situation. Rob had him page through a few screens and compared them to a few screens he was watching live. His screen showed someone in the middle of a very large transaction, at the AYS office.

Rob advised Al to stay at the computer terminal but get Chuck and Ron back to the office as quickly as possible.

Ron, Chuck, Mike and Kelly rushed back to the office and caught up with Rob. He told them he had just finished tracking the source of the transaction. It was coming from a network drop in the storage closet very close to Chuck's office.

They made their way to the room, quietly opened the door and could hear keys of a keyboard typing rapidly. Mike and Kelly quietly made their way into the room as Chuck and Ron followed closely behind them.

Mike and Kelly were in shock when they saw who it was and had to rush to stop her from typing. They each grabbed an arm to stop her and Chuck heard another very familiar voice.

He looked at the woman who was sitting at the keyboard and exclaimed, "Millie, my oldest and dearest friend, how could you?"

Ron added, "Millie? I thought you were afraid of computers, you panic over anything with more than two buttons." Then he remembered the books he saw at her desk, "Cobalt for dummies and C + + and you," the ones she said were left there by someone and were now paperweight's, it made sense now.

Chuck looked at Millie and asked her, "How could you Millie, after all these years together?" Then sat down and had the look of a man who just lost his best friend.

Millie replied in a voice that was filled with anguish and frustration from working for someone who had taken her for granted for too long. She fought through her tears and replied, "Please, you've given me a hundred reasons why I should turn on you Chuck! You're the most self absorbed, self centered man I've ever worked for. Do you remember all the times I've come to you for help, all the times I needed off. Do you know what it's like to miss my grandchildren's birthdays, my husband's retirement party, my anniversaries? All so you could go golfing in the afternoon or some other nonsense.

For the second time that day, Chuck looked at Ron for support. Chuck's eyes were also welling up with tears but again Ron replied, "You've brought all this on yourself Chuck, I've been trying to tell you since I've been here. Don't you see a pattern here?"

Ron could see that Millie and Chuck were both truly crushed by all that had happened. Ron asked Chuck,

"Are you alright, we should probably get you back to your office now, you've had a rough day."

Ron then turned to Millie, gave her a long hug and admitted that he understood where she was coming from. Unfortunately there was probably not much he could do to help her.

Millie replied through her tears, "This was my last shot at retiring Ron, by next month I would've had enough put away to quit this place, that's all I ever wanted," and wiped away her tears.

She added, "I can't continue working for that man, I'd rather be dead, do you hear me Chuck, I'd rather be dead than work for you, you're a horrible human being!" She pointed at Chuck and continued, "You reap what you sow Chuck, the sooner you learn that the better!"

As the Police arrived, Ron and Chuck returned to Chuck's office. Once Chuck had collected himself he seemed most concerned about hiding all of this from the home office. The VP's, upper management and the entire region were expected to swarm into the office tomorrow. The district was up for an award for having the best numbers; Chuck knew he had to hide all of this somehow.

Ron added, "You've already swept too much under the carpet Chuck, you can't keep managing like this. Someone's going to find out eventually!"

Chuck replied, "I've done alright so far, we have to cover this up Ron, please just do as I ask."

Ron shook his head and wondered how it would all end.

The following day, Ron met with Chuck in his office bright and early. Ron had arranged for Renee to cover for Millie in high hopes that Renee could take over Millie's job if the dispatch problem worsened.

Ron was trying to persuade Chuck to come clean about the third party service problem they had uncovered. He did a rough calculation and determined that close to a million dollars in parts were stolen and stashed in Jacks office.

Ron added, "You can't hide that for long Chuck, when it's finally uncovered your going to have a lot of explaining to do."

Ron was about to advise Chuck about a second option and how they could spin it so he looked like a hero when suddenly there was a knock on Chuck's door.

Chuck added, "Not a word of this Ron!"

Ron looked at Chuck and thought, "How the hell did this guy become a manager?"

The door opened and one of the VP's came in and told Chuck, "Chuck, how's my favorite son in law?" and shook Chuck's hand.

Ron rolled his eyes and thought to himself, "That explains everything!"

The VP and Ron introduced themselves and shook hands, the VP added, "I've been hearing a lot of great things about you Ron. Chuck has told me all about how he's taken you under his wing, showed you how to whip that team of screwballs into shape. From the numbers I've seen you've done very well, very well indeed."

Ron replied, "Yeah, Chucks quite a character alright. To be honest I'm still trying to figure out how this place runs with him here, I can't keep up with him."

The VP looked puzzled and asked, "You mean when he's not here, right?"

Ron looked at Chuck with a grin and replied, "I guess."

The VP then asked Chuck, "So where's Millie this morning, I don't believe I've ever heard of her taking a day off."

Chuck replied, "I'm not sure, I'm still waiting for her to call."

Again Ron looked at Chuck, who had a very concerned look on his face and Ron decided enough was enough; someone had to save the old man from himself.

Ron added, "Chuck was just saying he wanted to get all the facts together before telling you but we're waiting for Millie to call us from the police station. Chuck and I have uncovered a third party service business operating in our area. I'm afraid Millie was part of it and is probably still in jail."

The VP looked at Chuck and replied, "Is this true, how long has this been going on?"

Chuck looked at Ron with a scowl and replied, "Uh, yeah, I'll let Ron explain some of the details but yes, I'm afraid so, very disappointing."

Ron went on to explain how it all unfolded, the detective work of his crew and Rob that had led to the arrests. The VP was amazed at the dollar amount of the parts stash and upset to learn that Sam and Millie were involved.

He added, "What about Sam's boy, I've heard nothing but good things about him, we have to take care of the boy, I hear he's a borderline genius."

Ron replied, "Genius? Collin is one of the most obnoxious little bastards I've ever met."

The VP replied, "I heard he's a very gifted technician, those types are usually like that. I hear it has to do with their minds working at a whole different level, they get frustrated when we can't keep up with them."

Ron responded, "Who do you get your information from? Collin has destroyed at least two machines, most of our customers hate his guts and refuse to allow him near their equipment, that kid is a disaster!"

The VP replied, "Chuck is that true?"

Chuck replied, "This is news to me but why are we talking so much about Collin, what about my dispatchers, will they have jobs tomorrow?"

The VP replied, "That's my son in law, always concerned for his people."

Ron thought to himself, "Where do they get these guy's from, ones dumber than the other."

The VP continued, "The overseas dispatch is almost a done deal, all of my counterparts are focused on one number, the money we can save from making the move."

Ron responded, "That's very short sighted sir, were going to lose a lot of customers over this."

The VP replied, "That remains to be seen at this time."

Ron added, "Please, while you're here, spend some time in the dispatch area, see how we work. Our regional specialist Rob has a phone line set up so you can listen in on our customers, dispatcher's and the overseas dispatchers. You've got to reconsider, our customers hate the overseas dispatch system and you're about to make a huge mistake."

They broke up their meting and were amazed when they opened Chuck's door. The office was more crowded than they had ever seen it. There were managers, specialists and techs from other districts as well as a lot of upper management people from the main office.

The VP added, " I think you guy's are in for a very long day, I'll take your suggestion though Ron and spend some time in the dispatch area. I'll need a full report with all the details about this third party business but nice job Chuck, Ron."

Chuck replied, "Why thank you Ed, you know me, always on top of things. I'll have that together for you as soon as possible."

After Ed left, Chuck looked at Ron with a scowl and told him, "I thought I told you not to say anything about all of this Ron!"

Ron replied, "You should be thanking me Chuck, I may have just saved you your job. Do you really think that losing a million dollars in parts would go unnoticed for long? At least now you look like you know what you're doing."

As he was leaving, Chuck overheard Ron mutter under his breath, "Always on top of things my ass!"

Chuck thought about it for a moment and said to himself, "Oh yeah, now I get it."

Ron headed to his office and found half of his crew waiting for him.

Al asked Ron, "Where've you been, you don't look very happy."

Ron replied, "Just making nice with Chuck and one of the VP's. Did you know Chuck's father in law is a Vice President with AYS?"

Al replied, "Sure, we all do."

Ron responded, "When were you planning on sharing that with me, that little piece of information would've made my job so much easier. It explains everything I ever needed to know about Chuck."

Al replied, "Sorry, I guess it never came up."

Ron then saw Dave and Daryl approach the VP and heard Dave yell out, "Uncle Ed, am I glad to see you!"

Ron looked at Al and added, "What is this place, Nepo depot!"

Ron shook his head and continued, "How's Renee holding up, doing dispatch and Millie's job?"

John replied, "She's doing ok so far, it's not like Millie ever really did anything." Al added, "Millie's been doing a lot more than any of us ever realized, can you believe that. She's pretends to be afraid of cell phones and computers but she's actually a programmer!"

Ron responded, "I still like Millie, I can see how working for a butt hole like Chuck for too long can do things to you. Look at Jack; he's probably a decent enough guy. I think this was all revenge, Chuck's sins of the past catching up with him, you know."

Just then Chuck barged through Ron's door along with a few of the corporate VP's. Many of them had heard about the dog pound before but unfortunately none of it was good. When Ron took over they were the worst rated team in the country and Ron wondered who he had pissed off to be put in charge of them. After firing a couple of the worst techs the uphill battle began. By now, Ron had come to really enjoy and respect his team.

Ron did his best to hammer the VP's about the dispatchers and told them, "You have no idea how important the bond between the techs, dispatchers and customers are. I see it everyday, when they're having a rough day they pull for each other, they're all part of a team. You're going to screw with that and lose it."

Ron was being blunt and to the point but didn't care, that's the way Ron had always been. The VP's told Ron, "Nothing has changed as of yet, decisions were still being made at this time."

Renee called Ron as the VP's were leaving and advised him that calls were backing up. The VP's listened as Ron and his techs devised a game plan with Renee to get through it.

As the techs were leaving, Ron told them, "Alright guys, lets clean up the open calls early today. I'll catch up with you at the meeting, say four o'clock."

After they left, Ron's phone rang, it was Angela. Even over the phone Ron could tell when she was getting ready to tell him something juicy, her voice just took on a certain tone when she was excited about something.

Ron replied, "I know this has to be something good, what's up my dear?"

Angela responded, "Do you have a TV anywhere, there's something on the news you have to see."

Ron said, "Not at the moment, the office is crawling with people today, what have you got for me?"

Angela explained, "I think your building buddy was busted today, seems she's more like a naughty neighbor."

Ron got up and looked out of his window; even from across the street he could see police all over his building buddy's office.

Angela added, "It looks like she was running a call girl ring from the office, they arrested a bunch of her clients as well."

They both had a good laugh and Ron added, "I'm sure glad I married a hottie like you baby, keeps me honest."

Angela replied, "Just wait till I get you home tonight stud, I'll have to reward you for behaving yourself."

Ron responded, "Do you still have that silver outfit I bought you."

Angela replied, "I do, I love what you're thinking right now."

They hung up and Ron was getting ready to head to the dispatch room when his phone rang again, this time it was Bill.

Bill explained, "Ron, I need your help friend."

Ron could hear a lot of noise in the background and asked, "Where the hell are you, Grand Central station?"

Bill replied, "I should be so lucky, I'm at the Police station. I need you to come and bail me out before anyone in the office finds out."

Ron responded, "You dirty dog, you were doing my building buddy weren't you?"

Bill replied, "I guess you heard the news, she was running a brothel over there. I really didn't know Ron, please believe me."

Ron replied, "You've got nothing to prove to me buddy, she's hot. If I weren't married I would've been over there myself. Was she worth it?"

Bill responded, "I wish I knew, the cops barged in before I even knew what was going on. Anyway, how soon can you get here?"

Ron headed to the precinct and bailed out Bill as well as Millie. The desk sergeant recognized him from the time he had to bail out Stu and commented, "You know, here at the midtown Hilton you qualify for our three for one package. The next overnight stay is on us, what kind of business are you running over there anyway?"

When Ron told him it was a copier company the sergeant replied, "Our copier is a piece of crap, why don't you send a sales rep over, maybe we can do business?"

As for Millie, Ron and Bill both felt terrible for her, she couldn't bear the thought of losing her retirement package. Ron explained that he would try to do something for her.

Ron and Bill headed back to work and joined in the chaos that had become their office for the day.

Bill continued hammering the VP's with the dispatch issue and Ron did his best to get his team through a hectic day.

It was around three o'clock when the techs got the call from Ron, "Permission granted to drop everything, let's party, you've all earned it!"

Mike met up with Brad, John and Kelly in front of the hotel in Times Square where the meeting was being held. As they entered the main party room they saw many new faces. Managers, techs and sales reps from other districts were on hand from all over the Northeast region.

Ron saw them and waved them over to a large table he reserved for his team. It was off to the side in a secluded area.

Ron told them, "If there's a crew anywhere that needs privacy it's us, besides, you guys worked your butts off for this, let's have some fun."

Ron slowly gathered his crew, the room was packed to capacity and had at least thirty large tables.

The meeting was called to order by one of the VP's who explained, "I am very proud of you all for your hard work this quarter, especially our Manhattan district who have come in with some of the best numbers ever."

Everyone applauded and some of Ron's guys started making their barking and howling noises. Ron looked at them and said, "Please tell me you guys haven't started drinking yet."

Some of the other teams looked over and shook their heads, a few made comments like, "Losers!"

John replied, "That's not what your girlfriend said last night."

Someone else yelled back at John, "You're Grandmother told me last night!"

Ron quietly chuckled, looked at John and told him, "Down boy, heel."

One of the other VP's took the podium and commented on the dispatch problem. He put up charts showing the cost's involved with running a localized dispatch area in its present form and explained the savings they could achieve by switching to an overseas operation.

At least half of the audience raised their hands to comment but the VP added, "There is nothing that will be decided in this meeting today, so we will not be accepting any questions on the issue. However, let it be known we have been studying the pros and cons carefully. This Manhattan district has given us great insight into the role and value of maintaining a localized dispatch and its importance on day-to-day operations.
With that, let's proceed with the award ceremony."

He brought up one of the VP's and introduced Chuck as the Manhattan District manager. Mike looked around the room and watched the other techs start prepping. Some had cue cards prepared for speeches they were expecting to give. The table of techs from Boston were all dressed in the sharpest suits, they were usually the ones who won these awards.

Al caught Mike looking over at the Boston table and told him, "Forget those knuckleheads." Al then pointed at Greg and added, "Remember what I told you about the best dressed guys, there's a table full of them over there. They fudge their numbers," he pointed at the big-shots and added, "They read those numbers," then pointed at the award plaques and said, "They give them those awards based on the bogus numbers. Who needs it? "

Mike looked up and saw Ron, Brad and John looking up at them and laughing. Ron put his hand to his ears, Brad put his hands over his eyes and John put his hands over his mouth. Al told him, "Hear no evil, see no evil and speak no evil."

Ron added, "Deaf, dumb and blind is more like it, I'll take working with you guys any day," then let out a bark.

And so it began, they started with the award for best attendance, then a few others. In no time at all everyone at the tables was starting to fall asleep until they announced, "The next award is for outstanding teamwork," then went on to describe a situation that a team had gone through.

They added, "Sales was close to losing a major account, it was only after sales, service and management pulled together and overcame great obstacles to save the account, then went even further and placed a number of new machines."

Mike and Brad looked at each other and John said, "Big deal, we did that too."

The VP continued, "From the Manhattan sales team, lets have a round of applause for Ivanna and Joyce."

As the applause broke out, the girls made their way to the podium.

Chuck added, "Lets also put our hands together for some of our techs, I was told none of this could have happened without their help, lets bring up Brad, John and Mike."

They were in shock for a moment but eventually made their way to the podium. Mike saw Gertie along the way, he grabbed her hand and got her to reluctantly join them.

Once at the podium, they all exchanged hugs and congratulations. The entire district was on their feet applauding and they could hear their dogs barking in the background.

As they returned to their seats they looked at Ron and made the hear, see and speak no evil sign. Ron told them, "Deaf dumb and blind is still more like it," then added,

"You made me proud guys, great job."

The VP continued, "The next award goes to the most improved territory. The winner is someone who has worked diligently to take a territory that was, well, there's no other way to put it but falling apart. This individual has turned both the equipment and customers around, we now want to award Mike from the crew who calls themselves the dog pound."

Mike stared in disbelief, Ron stood up and applauded followed by the rest of the dog-pound. On the way up to the podium he heard his dogs in the background and couldn't recall ever feeling so good, it really came out of nowhere.

On the way back he saw Joyce, who looked at him, put her hand on her heart and mouthed the words, "Way to go stud," then blew him a kiss.

He suddenly felt that same feeling for Joyce he had on his first day back at the sales office.

Mike made his way back to his team and they were as excited as he was.

Greg tried to tell him, "See Mike, you should thank me, I left you in great shape, some of that award belongs to me you know."

John replied, "Yeah Greg, more like it's easy to improve on something when you start with crap."

Mike added, "I guess I can say I couldn't have done it without you Greg."

Ron added, "Wait till Gary and Bernice hear you're a hero now Mike."

They all went on laughing and joking for a few minutes, then Chuck announced the next award. Chuck went on to say, "The next award is one that upper management looks on with great importance as it directly affects the bottom line and revenue. The next award is for the fewest parts used in a territory. The recipient must be a very resourceful individual to have received this recognition. The award goes to Greg, from the dog pound again."

Greg sprang up immediately and raised his arms. As he made his way to the podium he looked like the Pope making his way through the masses. Ron and the guys were cracking up with laughter, Al was laughing so hard he had tears in his eyes.

After Greg returned to the table there was no stopping him, his ego was out of control. He told Mike he should hold on to his award as well, seeing as it was part his.

He added, "See, I actually received two awards tonight."

Then told Ron, "I'd make a great assistant manager for you Ron, I can start Monday," then tried splitting up his territory amongst the techs so he could start Monday.

Ron replied, "No, I'm good Greg, if I needed someone to do nothing I'd talk to one of the VP's over there."

The guy's got tired of hearing Greg and started bombarding him with balled up napkins and anything else they could find. Eventually he couldn't take it anymore and left the table for a while.

The award presentation continued and eventually they got to the best group in the region award. They watched the Boston techs begin standing up and start un-wrinkling their suits. A couple of them looked over at the dogs, one pointed, shook his head and laughed after saying something to one of his teammates. The other teammate held his hand to his head and formed the letter "L" for losers.

The VP started his introduction of the winning group. He said, "This year's winner is probably the most spirited bunch of individuals I've ever met. Although they're a little unorthodox, there is no denying their dedication to their customers and the success of the company, let's bring up the dogs."

Ron was in total shock and looked out with a blank stare, for all of two seconds. The rest of the team sprang up and began giving each other high fives then started hugging one another. Ron finally snapped out of his shock and joined in the celebration.

As they made their way to the podium, John got close enough to the Boston tech who was flashing the "L" and told him, "Yeah bitch, you lost to losers, what does that make you."

The guy said nothing, their entire table was quiet. They had won so many times they never thought they could lose, especially to a group of techs they despised.

Ron and his techs eventually made it to the front and received their awards. It took awhile though, they didn't realize it but in Manhattan they were beginning to be respected by some of the other groups and each one of those groups stopped them along the way.

The VP continued, "I've been watching you guys," then turned to Kelly and added, "And you my dear." He then addressed the group, "Do you realize in the last year all that you have accomplished? Last year you had the worst numbers in the country, customer satisfaction and equipment reliability were the worst I've ever seen. This year a survey showed your customers loved their equipment and service. So long as I have you all up here, let me give the final award for best service manager in the region to Ron."

The dogs went wild and it took a few minutes before anyone who wasn't up front already to see Ron. First the techs surrounded him, then some of the other teams and sales reps came up to congratulate him. He looked up briefly and saw Brad, John and Mike flash the hear no evil, see no evil and speak no evil sign.

When it finally quieted down, Ron told the crowd how much he loved and respected his techs and never could have turned the group around without their support. He then let out a howl followed by the rest of the dogs.

Even Chuck looked at Ron, held up his fist and said, "Woof!"

The meeting continued on after that for a couple of hours. After the formal stuff was over everyone ate, drank and had fun. It wasn't the kind of place you could really get loose though so towards the end Ron looked at his guy's and said, "Rosie's?"

Just then, Chuck and two of the VP's approached the podium. Chuck picked up the microphone, which came on with a loud humming noise and easily got everyone's attention.

Ron told his techs, "Oh-oh, they sobered up, how much you want to bet they're going to take away our awards?"

Chuck continued, "We were just contacted by the home office and wanted to share some exciting news with you. I won't mince words and bore you, it has been decided that dispatch in its present form will remain intact."

The entire room erupted in applause and excitement, everyone found the nearest dispatcher and gave them hug's and high fives.

The dogs looked all over for Renee, they found her on the phone with her mom sharing the news. They didn't realize it but Renee and her mom were going to sell their house and move if she had lost her job. As they surrounded Renee, she told her mom, "I really have to go," and hung up. The guy's all hugged her at once and Renee broke into tears then told them, "I love you guys."

They spread the word that the party was heading to Rosie's and left the district meeting.

It was a Friday and Rosie's was already jumping when they arrived. Al got a hold of Robin and asked if there was a table anywhere.

She told them, "I have a group just leaving, come on."

Just as they started getting comfortable, Joyce and Ivanna came in followed by Chuck and a few of the home office VP's. They all gathered at the dog's table and quickly overcrowded it. Eventually the people at the surrounding tables had to get up and leave. As more and more AYS people came in they eventually took over half of Rosie's.

The waitresses were glad to see them and Robin told them, "It's about time you guys showed up, these customers are being cheap tonight," and looked right at a table full of guy's who were nursing their drinks, then added, " I can finally make some money."

Ron and Chuck overheard Robin and each gave her a hundred bucks followed by two of the VP's and Ivanna who chipped in fifty apiece. They told her, "No matter what, keep the drinks coming for everybody, let us know when we spent that, then threw another fifty and told her that was hers."

Robin looked at her tray, then the table full of guys who were nursing their drinks and told them, " Alright, you heard the man, get the hell out of here you cheap bastard's, we have a party going on here," and started removing their drinks from the table.

Robin looked at Ron and added, "When are you hiring? I want to work for you guys. What is it someone's birthday?"

Al started telling Robin about all that had happened that day.

Robin replied, "I get it, you want to keep them drunk before they change their minds. They must have drank a lot to give you guy's awards."

Ron replied, "Keep talking like that and you'll be taking my job."

Robin headed to the bar and started getting everyone their drinks.

Amanda the shooter girl made her way to their section and Ron got her started on the VP's. Brad and John watched as Amanda worked her magic, she had the VP's toasted in no time. As she mixed the shooters, her butt always had the sexiest jiggle. One of the VP's kept trying to put his hands on her and it was becoming comical to watch. Amanda would give it a swat once in awhile at first, but she had a more permanent approach that always worked. Everyone watching knew it would stop once she started pumping him with double shots and showed him her necktie trick.

Mike was listening to John throw out a riddle about a brothel at the top of a mountain. He asked, "There are these three guys, one is heading up the mountain, one is at the top of the mountain and the third guy is coming down the mountain, what are their nationalities?"

Joyce had come by just as John asked the question. Joyce cut right in, "The guy heading up the mountain must be Russian, wouldn't you be, rushing?" and looked at Mike.

Mike replied "Well maybe, if it were you at the top."

The crowd collectively gave a, "Whhhoooaaa."

Brad reminded them about Mike's new commitment to Gary.

Joyce looked at Mike with a hurt look and obviously thought he was gay.

She said, "Oh, I had no idea Mike," and quickly walked away.

Mike went after her as she headed out the front door.

Mike yelled out, "Joyce, please, stop!"

She turned around, still with a hurt look and replied, "What Mike!"

Mike had feelings for Joyce since day one but had accepted Al's advice about office romances. He couldn't help it though and now knew Joyce felt the same way.

Mike continued, "Joyce, I'm not gay, I've never been gay, in fact," then paused, "I really have strong feelings for you, I have for some time now." He put his arms around her, looked into her eyes and they kissed, finally.

At first Joyce seemed reluctant but quickly went with her feelings. As they separated, Joyce looked into Mike's eyes and told him, "I've been waiting a long time for that you know."

Mike responded, "Was it worth the wait?"

Joyce smiled and replied, "Not really," then grabbed him and gave him a more passionate kiss. She added, "But that will have to do for now, I don't want to spoil you for Gary."

Mike looked at Joyce and told her, "Oh stop," in a feminine voice and continued, "I wonder what Gary's doing right now."

Joyce shot back very quickly, "Himalayan."

Mike joked and told her, "You mean he got over me that quick, that little whore."

Joyce laughed and told him, "No, not Gary, Johns riddle, the guy at the top of the mountain, Himalayan, he's Himalayan."

She grabbed Mike by the hand and they rushed back into Rosie's. The techs figured out that the guy coming down the mountain was Finish but they were still stumped by the guy at the top.

Brad looked at Mike, noticed lipstick on his cheek and asked, "So what have you been doing."

Joyce shouted at John, "Himalayan."

Brad looked at Mike and replied, "Good for you Mike, that must have been a quick one," he put his hand on Mike's shoulder and added, "I never had you pegged for a minuteman there Mike."

Joyce looked at Brad and told him, "No not us you boob, the guy at the top of the mountain, he's Himalayan."

John replied, "You're right, that's it, but that scares me Joyce, it's usually the perverts who get that one."

The whole table cracked up laughing.

Al looked at Mike with a smile and said, "Mike, what did you do?"

Kelly pinched Al's arm and said, "Leave them alone, they look cute together!"

Mike replied, "I couldn't help it Al, I really like Joyce, a lot."

Al admitted they really did make a cute couple and wished them luck.

They looked over toward the bar and noticed Amanda walking towards them, counting her money. Mike pointed to the bar, the VP who couldn't keep his hands off of Amanda's butt now had his neck and hands tied to the bar with his necktie. They could overhear him talking to the other VP who was trying to untie him, he was very drunk and slurring his speech.

As she walked by Mike she looked up and cleaned the lipstick off of his face and told him in her sweet Spanish accent, "It's about time sweetie, I always knew you and Joyce would get together," and kept walking.

Al added, "You have to teach us that necktie trick Amanda."

She turned to Al and replied, "You could hurt someone with that, I'll see."

Just then someone started playing, "Who let the dog's out," on the jukebox.

Everyone from AYS started singing along with the music and eventually most of Rosie's was getting into it as well.

Ron was at his usual spot on the second floor taking in the show with Chuck and Bill. He decided that this would be a good time to remind Chuck about the bet they had made when Chuck was trying to convince him to stay.

Chuck had agreed to give up his corner office if Ron could turn the dogs around. Chuck knew it was a long shot so he figured it was a safe bet and went along with it, never realizing that Ron could pull it off.

Not only did Ron pull it off and turn them around but he now had the best team in the region, possibly the country.

Ron told Chuck, "Should we start swapping our furniture around tonight or you want to wait till Monday morning?"

Chuck cringed and became defensive, then replied, "What are you talking about?"

Ron responded, "Don't go getting all Alzheimer's on me now Chuck, you remember our agreement!"

Bill added, "I've been waiting to hear what that was about," then pointed downstairs to Al and motioned him to come upstairs.

Chuck continued pretending to not know what Ron was talking about but Ron was ready for him. Since day one when Chuck suckered Ron into coming to New York, Ron had vowed to never let Chuck get the better of him again.

Ron replied, "Chuck, have you ever heard the saying, "Fool me once, shame on you, fool me twice shame on me?"

Al and John had just arrived upstairs as Chuck replied, "No but that's a catchy phrase, I have to remember that one. What does that have to do with my office though?"

Ron reached into his pocket and pulled out the voice recorder from the nanny cam he kept in his office. Ron hit play and everyone heard Ron and Chuck's conversation from that memorable day when he agreed to stay in New York.

Chuck listened and replied, "I must have agreed to that under duress Ron, surely you know I'll never give up my office. Like I always say.."

Ron cut him off and added, "What Chuck, what do you always say, Screw your managers and everyone else around you?

Bill added, "No, I think its life is like a box of chocolates, sometimes I get confused and take the ex-lax by mistake!"

Al replied, "No, what I heard him say was the last time I thought this hard I clogged the toilet! That's what it was!"

Ron responded again, "Give it up Chuck, haven't you learned anything?"

Bill added, "You can't weasel out of something like this Chuck, a bet's a bet!"

John said, "You big woos!"

Chuck scowled and looked directly at John.

John turned and added, "Who the hell said that?"

Everyone but Chuck laughed briefly then they all stared at Chuck and replied, "Well, now what?"

Chuck suddenly started feeling light headed, he put his hand to his chest and seemed ready to pass out.

Ron and Bill held him up and got a young couple to give up their table so Chuck could sit down. They brought him a glass of water and were going to call an ambulance but Chuck insisted he was alright.

Ron added, "There's only one thing I want more than your corner office Chuck, if you agree to it I'll let you off the hook, this time."

Chuck looked up at Ron and asked, "This can't be good but what is it?"

Ron explained that he had bailed Millie out of jail and that she was extremely upset about losing her retirement package."

Chuck replied, "So, she deserves to lose it, after what she did to me!"

Ron responded, "If you weren't such a butthole all the time maybe she wouldn't have did what she did. Anyway, if you agree to drop all charges against her and reinstate her retirement package I'll give up on your office."

Chuck scowled and again seemed ready to faint but replied, "I'd rather not go down that road. I'm pretty sure corporate has a special stipend I can use to compensate you Ron, I'll look into it first thing Monday morning."

They all laughed and Ron replied, "You've really got to get rid of that line Chuck, it's older than dinosaur turd!"

Chuck responded, "Are you trying to say you don't believe me?"

Ron replied, "Oh I believe you Chuck, it's your words that lack integrity."

Chuck looked confused and thought for a moment, then asked, "If I don't press charges on Millie you'll give up this nonsense about my office!"

Ron added, "She keeps her retirement package too!"

Chuck thought for a moment and finally agreed to let Millie off the hook.

Ron was silent for a moment and everyone could tell that Ron was upset, he really wanted the office and deserved it after all he had been through.

Ron finally smiled and told Chuck, "That's really the right thing to do."

The party continued for awhile but slowly everyone started heading home.

Chuck had remained behind and was talking to his father in law at the bar. Bert could hear the conversation and heard Chuck gloating over how he had screwed Ron out of getting his office. Chuck laughed and added, "And the award for best acting goes to, me! I can fake a fainting spell with the best of them Ed. You want to see what a heart attack looks like," and laughed. He added, "Imagine that, the imbecile really believed I'd give up my office!"

Bert immediately picked up the phone and called Al, who called Bill and then the dogs.

Chapter 9 - The End

Ron arrived at the office, bright and early Monday morning. He was feeling pretty good about himself and his techs winning awards for their hard work. He felt even better about Millie even though she had to sign an agreement to stay away from any corporate networks. At least she could retire now and Ron couldn't wait to call her the minute he got to his office.

Still he thought, "That corner office would've been nice."

He got to his office door and saw a sign on it that read, "Do not enter!" and another that read, "See Chuck for details." He tried to open the door but it was locked. He made his way to Chuck's office and knocked but there was no answer. He opened the door and all at once his techs and Bill yelled, "Surprise!"

Ron was stunned and at first didn't get it until he looked around the office, It was filled with his stuff. Bill filled him in on what had happened and added, "We owe you this Ron, for all that you've done for us it's the least we can do. We couldn't let Chuck screw you out of his agreement, we all pitched in and moved your things over the weekend.

Ron asked Bill, "How did you get the old man to go along with this?"

Bill then explained how Chuck had tried to play him with the phony heart attack routine and how Bert had heard the whole thing. Then he pulled Ron over and quietly whispered in his ear, "Remember our building buddy, Chuck was one of her best clients. She told me so and I threatened to tell his wife the whole thing if he didn't man up, grow a pair and live up to his agreement. He made me promise not to tell anyone but this seems like a fairer exchange, nothing like getting screwed twice for the price of one, eh!"

Ron then laughed and thanked Bill as well as his dogs for giving up their weekend for him.

Bill did his best Don Corleone impression from the Godfather and added, "There may come a day when I will ask a favor of you, this will be a favor you cannot refuse me."

Ron replied, "Almost anything, just don't ask me to take those smucks off of your hands."

Bill added, "Oh come on Ron, not even for the corner office?"

Ron's techs picked up any paper they could find, balled it up and started bombarding Bill with it while yelling, "No! Get the hell out of here!"

Bill replied, "I'm going to dump them off on you sooner or later!"

They all finally left after awhile, Ron called Angela and told her all about his new office. Angela was overjoyed to hear the good news, she couldn't stand the thought of Chuck getting over on him again, especially after all that they had been through.

Angela had been in the backyard with Katie when he called. Their worries over goose poopies was now history too, they had taken their neighbors suggestion and bought Katie a small dog they named Missy. The dog was a miniature collie and was a pro at getting rid of geese, she and Katie were becoming inseparable and the dog was just so cute.

Chuck was busy trying to settle into Ron's old office but was having problems. He refused to give up any of his furniture and had no room at all. Still, he kept his indoor putting range even though he could now putt only a foot in front of him, it used to be eighteen feet. Chuck was miserable!

Ron's team now had bragging rights and were the best team in the city, the dogs had finally achieved the respect they deserved and it felt great!

As for Mike, he was now considered a seasoned tech and was really enjoying the job. His territory was running well and he had finally gotten a handle on most of his difficult customers. He and Joyce were now seeing each other and they both agreed to take it slow for now.

He had just left Active Graphics and was going to meet up with Al and wait for a part from the new parts delivery guy, then go to lunch at Liberty park. He wondered what ever happened to Sam and Collin but really not that much and accepted it as his luck.

He spotted Al, they shook hands and Al told him he had some strange news for him. Al added, "You'll never believe who I saw at Sloppy copy. Gil hired Oscar and Lyzette, Oscar is now one of their operators and Lyzette is trying out for a mid level managers job. The whole time I was there she was berating Oscar, the poor guy. All Gil kept talking about was how hot he was for Lyzette, he says he's in love with her. I tried to tell him how crazy she is and he said, "I don't care, the more crazy the better, I love that crazy bitch!"

Mike replied, "Is that really a surprise, we knew all along he wasn't right." Mike saw the delivery van approaching them and added, "This is going to be good, maybe I'll actually have a part handed to me instead of thrown at my head."

As the van got closer, the part came flying out of the window just as it always had. Mike and Al looked at one another and wondered how it could be. Sam was still in jail and could never get his old job back. Who could be driving the van and carrying on his tradition?

As they watched the part, they noticed it was flying away from them and towards a bunch of motorcycles that were parked at the curb. The part slammed into one of the bikes and then the light turned red, the van was trapped at the light and the bikers started surrounding it.

The bikers started rocking the van and then Mike heard a familiar voice from inside. He looked at Al and said, "It couldn't be, Collin?"

Mike asked Al, "You think they'll flip it?"

Al replied, "I don't want to be here if they do, come on, let's get out of here, we'll find your part somewhere else. So they headed to the park and enjoyed the rest of the day.

As for Ron, he looked out of his new corner office window and thought, "I love this job!"

The author, Michael S. Modzelewski has drawn on his thirty years of experience as a technician in the printing industry to create a colorful cast of characters and comic situations.

Have you ever thought to yourself, "I could write a book with all the weird stuff I've been through?"

He has, and he hopes you've enjoyed reading this book about it.

Please Email all inquiries and comments regarding this book to AtYourServiceCopiers@Yahoo.com

Made in the USA
Middletown, DE
26 November 2019